STACKER

Stuart Webb

"All modern revolutions have ended in reinforcement of the power of the state."
Albert Camus

Stuart Webb was born in Cambridge in 1985. He studied Creative Writing and Film & Television Studies at the University of Derby, graduating in 2006.
At thirty he fled to Cromer on the East Coast of Britain to avoid paying off the mental and emotional debts of his twenties.
Stuart lives alone with a Yucca Plant called Spike. He enjoys sunglasses and red trousers.

CHAPTER ONE

I am Stacker and this is what I do;

I work graveyards at the Megamarket on the edge of town, midnight until seven. Five days a week. This is not how anybody imagines their life is going to turn out.

It began the Christmas after I graduated and it just never ended. It wasn't supposed to be like this, it was supposed to be a temporary contract. The plan was to stack the shelves through December and half of January to get some money for the Christmas and post-Christmas pubs. In the new year I was to look for something proper and respectable over which to sweat my days and dedicate my life. But the Suits had other designs on me. I was taking a lot of Speed those days and anyway I was naturally enthusiastic and every morning my aisle was filled up tight and square. They didn't want me to leave.

I didn't leave.

The problem is this; the work is easy and I don't really want anything substantial from or for my life. I just want to be and to smell the existential dread. Every January they give us a 10% bonus which is enough to clear the debts of the previous year and on we go. I don't want a career and I don't want a family. I live in a bedsit and I drink wine in my pants, there is no need to change. There is no want to better myself, I mean, if you can't be Bob Dylan why be anything? I am Stacker and this is how I live.

The big hand scrapes around the clock picking up minutes and then dumping them out behind it. The stock comes in on cages that come in on the back of big Megamarket branded Lorries. The cages are lined up in the warehouse in rows corresponding to the aisles. The job of a Stacker is to fetch a cage from out back and work the stock up and down the aisle. The trick of the job is to take your mind out of it; let your arms and legs work, let your hands and feet guide. You can make it through a shift easy enough if your brain is elsewhere.

You daydream.

Working graveyard means there are no customers to get in your way and no Suits to tether you down. The Suits like to keep regular hours pretending they work in an office or something. The Team Leaders run the show overnight. My Team Leader is a drip of milk called Samuel Walters, always Samuel never Sam, a real company man. He gets off on wearing his Team Leader badge and carrying his clipboard and breaking balls and slapping wrists.

"Pet food, come here." Samuel calls you by the aisle you're working, I don't know why. It's his little kick and I couldn't care less, sometimes I can't even remember my name. I'm on my knees cramming cat litter onto the bottom shelf and look up to him standing at the top of the aisle, clipboard in hand lights reflecting off his glasses.

"Yes Samuel." I say and walk up the aisle towards him wiping my hands down the front of my apron, he makes no effort to meet me, just stands there drumming his pen against his clipboard. Some days I feel like sticking my safety knife down his throat. "What's up?"

"Management are having a big drive on uniform standards. You need to do up your top button and tuck your shirt in." Samuel was the sort of guy that wet dreamed of being middle management.

"Sam, its half past three in the morning, there are no customers here…"

"My name is Samuel and that is beside the point. It's about representing the company. Don't shoot the messenger." He smiles his weak, sickly smile and blinks, his watery eyes magnified behind his thick glasses. So I button up and tuck my shirt in and shake my head at the stupidity of it all and Samuel pisses off on his way.

The actual work is alright, you send your mind off on vacant space adventures and most of the other bottom rung workers are okay but the people like Samuel can be a bit of a drag. I guess you get them in all walks, the sticklers; the straight edged kind. The people that get off on rules and clipboards and top buttons.

These are the people that climb the ladders.

At four I go and smoke a cigarette in the shelter at the back of the yard. The moon is up and the clouds are the colour of dead teeth and everything is blanketed in quiet. Inside the shop we are all drones but under this sky some of us are poets.

I used to come out on these smoke breaks with old man Junker and we'd take turns swigging whatever was in his flask, usually some cheap blend own label stuff and then we'd crunch down half a packet of mints on the way back inside. Junker died in the fall of last year. I was happy for him. He was an old half German dog with a busted up, pockmarked face. "This is a face that's lived." He would say and chuckle thickly through the stained stumps of his teeth. He was a lot of things; a drunk, a wife beater, a bastard but he knew the measure of most and he never took any of it too serious.

Now I smoke on my own but I think of Junker up there somewhere beyond the bruised sky, up in the eternal dive bar and I don't feel so pissed off and alone. Reminds me to not take any of it too seriously.

Upstairs in the canteen Myers and Skin Tom are playing pool with the one good cue stick and Zeus is miking whatever meal he has pulled from the vendor. The television is on twenty-four-hour news with the sound down, broken subtitles pop and flex and roll for anyone interested enough. I get myself a Coke and sit down in front of it.

The Middle East is exploding, fragments of it are flying off every day, storms of dust and sand and blood and fire. People blast across a continent and for what? To drag everybody else down. This thing we call religion, it's dangerous and it's got the death rattle in its throat. It's going to be the end of us all. The third world war, when it finally arrives will be fought over fairy tales and oil with paedophile preachers screaming us forward, hysterical and hopeless.

And the smiles in the suits are too clean and neat and I can smell their bullshit even with the sound down. Full of we propose and we admire. This is why I sleep during the day. This is why I keep the sound down.

Myers pops the white ball clean off the table and into the glass of the vendor and laughs stupidly. The glass is strong and takes it without a crack or scuff and for a moment I wish I was the glass in a vending machine. I slap myself in the face for thinking such a dead end thought and take a sip of my Coke.

Five thirty-seven and I'm imagining banging nails into Christ's bony heretic hands. These are the sort of thoughts that you think when you haven't been thinking for a while. I flatten out the packing box for economy dog biscuits and shove it into the green sack that's hanging off the back of the morning's last cage. The sack is filled to over spilling so I uncouple it and take it, swinging lazily through the double doors at the back of the shop and head towards the industrial sized cardboard compactor.

As I tip the cardboard into the guts of the machine I think about climbing in myself and just waiting.

"How are you getting on?" Samuel appears behind me looking flustered as he always does towards the end when the fear of not meeting targets is looming and real.

"All done Sam; just the face up to go." And I shut the compactor door and push the button that brings down the big ram on everything inside. You can hear the cardboard creak and buckle. It sounds like an abattoir. Sam ignores being called Sam and says; "Good, good. Remember to face across off sales and everything facing forward."

"Okay Sam." I say and he scampers off to bother some other schmuck on the bottom rung.

This is the killer part of the job and it takes the last hour without fail. At least when you're stacking the job is broken up into component parts. Face up is unrelenting. Starting on one side you work your way up the aisle and these aisles are about half a mile long and then you move to the other side and come all the way back down. Nobody needs that many varieties of dog food and kitty shitter.

The hour stretches cruelly but eventually it yields. Outside the grey morning is spitting, the summer has been a wash out and is subsiding weakly into autumn. On my way out I buy a four pack of cold Budweiser and leave saying goodbye to no one, passing the day's first shoppers on my way.

Sitting in the half shelter of the bus stop at the bottom of the car park I drink the first beer of the day. Watching the rest of the world on their way to work with their headlights and brake lights refracting in the rain is the mornings one moment of triumph.

The first beer becomes the second beer and I'm halfway down it when the number seven swings in with its pneumatic brakes hissing and steaming. The doors wheeze open and a selection of the young and the old and the hopeless file out. I stand up and go to get on. The driver sees my open can and says; "You can't come on here with an open drink."

"Seriously?" I ask him, the rain is harder now and it pastes my hair to my face in cold swathes.

"Yes. Seriously."

"What if it was a Coke?"

"It's not a Coke." He looks at me like the fat, pissed off bus driver that he is, "I haven't got time for this, either put it down and get on or don't."

"Whatever, man." I say, "I'll walk." And I give him the finger as the doors crunch back together and the bus pulls back into the inching traffic.

CHAPTER TWO

My mum puts a cup of tea on the kitchen table in front of me and sits down opposite with her Mum of the Year cup filled with milky coffee. We are jammed down one end, the majority of table space given over to boxes, most of which are unopened, all of which have been ordered from the shopping channel.

"Your brother called at the weekend." She says, "Says he's doing very well over there, very busy he says. Getting into the season now apparently; did you know that Christmas time over there is during the summer? Imagine that." Her eyes get that faraway sheen as she imagines it.

"Good for him." I say. "Is he planning to visit anytime soon?"

"He didn't say. He said he was busy"

"Yeah, you said that." Robert went travelling round Australia four years ago and loved it so much he stayed. He got a job in a bar on Bondi beach which was owned by some old boy expat. Apparently he runs the place now.

"Diana was there in ninety six, you know? I would love to go one day." Mum says between blowing sips of coffee. My mother is obsessed with all things Princess Diana, says she was the last of the fairy tale princesses; a real queen of hearts. I think she was a slut.

"Why don't you go? It would do you good. Go and see Robert for a couple of weeks."

"Oh, darling I can't afford to do something like that."

"You could if you stopped buying stuff off the tele. You don't even open half of it mum." I say looking around.

"Yes but I might need it one day, you never know. That's what your father used to say."

"Yes but he was talking about light bulbs and fuse wire, not tea trays and cookie jars." But I know and she knows that there is no point in trying to make a conversation out of it.

When I was ten years old my father tried to hang himself. He was only partially successful and has been in a coma ever since. Despite the fact that he wrote a letter in which he was very clear that it was actually a genuine act of suicide, my mum was unable to accept it and despite the fact that by all accounts he is and will remain in a "vegetative state" she refuses to give permission to switch him off. He now resides in the Haywood home for the chronically fucked and fucked up.

"I'm going to feed the birds." I say and tip the last of the tea down my throat.

"Okay darling, thank you. I'm just going to be in the other room."

"Okay mum."

My father used to feed the birds like it was his duty, my mum never bothers. Every now and then I go out and do it, mainly out of some misplaced sense of duty towards the old man, not that he will ever know.

The grass is thick and long and too wet to cut. The garden is overgrown and unloved. Mum says she just hasn't the time to take care of these things and anyway, she says, it all seems so insignificant. Pigeons and Tits alight on the fence as I open the shed door, as if they know what's coming; like the opening of the door is a remembered signifier of food from back when the old man did it every day.

When the feeding is done I go back into the house and find mum sitting in dad's old chair watching the news. The living room is a kingdom of sad boxes. My father had been in a coma for one week when Princess Diana died. There are no cushions with his face embroidered on them.

A girl gets beaten to death on a beach in Thailand.

A fifteen year old kid burns down a dog home.

Another journalist gets beheaded.

My mum watches the news blankly saying; "What a world we live in. What a world."

"The birds are fed."

"Thank you, love." She says without looking up and suddenly she looks very old and very tired. I sit down on the sofa between a blender and a Princess Diana tea set.

"How is work?" She says.

"It's alright, it's a supermarket; it doesn't change." There was no dream job in the media after University there was just a self-carved rut.

"Have you seen your dad recently?"

"Not for a while."

"You should go and see him, he'll like that."

"Okay mum."

And then we sit in silence for a bit. I tell her that I'm tired and need to go to bed and she calls me a vampire and I leave.

CHAPTER THREE

I know I am dreaming. I've dreamt this before.

I'm outside the factory with its coal black walls and smoke. The gate is open and I'm in the yard surrounded by skinny faceless men dressed in identical black suits, white shirts, black ties. Everyone is shuffling forward. The moon is fat and white and scored by shards of cloud.

Inside now and I take my place on one of the long benches that stretch further than I can see. Everyone pauses and I become aware of the giant ticking clock face at the far end of the chamber and an alarm cuts through the quiet.

I wake up and silence my phone and for a long time I just lie in my bed and don't move. I have a text from Mike saying "Pint tonight?" I say "Sure." And look around the room for cigarettes.

They called it a Studio Apartment at the estate agents. It sounds more upmarket than Bedsit I guess. I have a bed and a beat-up couch and a television. They called it a kitchenette at the estate agents but it's nothing more than a hob and a sink and a microwave and everything is thick with grime.

I tap ash into an empty wine bottle and sit on the edge of the bed. Outside it's still raining. Mike texts saying "Cody's?" and I say "OK." Cody's is a cheap bar on the way to work. I go into the bathroom and take a long hot shower until the mirror steams over and the air is wet and the paint on the walls begins to peel.

Mike is already in there by the time I walk through the door, sitting at the bar halfway down a pint glass. I sit down next to him and wait for Big Steve to come over. Mike does something in finance. We live in different worlds. Sometimes you're only friends with someone because you've known them so long.

Big Steve comes over and I ask him for two bottles of Budweiser. The clock says eight. Cody's is always quiet on a Tuesday; everything is quiet on a Tuesday. We stay at the bar.

"Happy Tuesday." He says and holds up his glass.

"Aren't they all?" I say back and we knock drinks.

"I was on the train this evening, getting back into town," he says, "and a skinhead handed me a flier about a Defence League demonstration this weekend at the Plaza. They're actually handing out fliers now. I couldn't believe it, man. I mean, isn't that illegal?"

"I don't know."

"And the most fucked up thing about it was the guy was wearing a suit."

"That is fucked up. How old was he?"

"Mid-twenties, maybe our age." Mike shakes his head and takes a long gulp. "It won't be long before those guys run the country."

"It's all falling apart." I agree with him. The Great in Great Britain has become ironic these days. Mike's phone vibrates loudly in his pocket and he takes it out saying; "Fucking thing vibrates as loud as it rings." He squints at it and his thumb dabs at the touch screen opening a text message.

"Can you remember life before mobile phones?"

"I can't remember anything before 9/11." He says. "And that's the truth." I grew up with Mike but our lives forked when it came to career paths. He taps out his reply and calls out; "When you're ready Steve." As he drains his glass and puts it back on the bar. Big Steve looks up from the Sports section and nods.

"Have you got to work tonight?" Mike asks me putting his phone back in his pocket. Big Steve makes his way over behind his massive stomach and reloads the pint glass. Mike puts a five on the bar.

"I work every night, man."

"What time?" And then; "Thanks Steve." As the pint is placed in front of him.

"Midnight. Same as every other time you ask me."

"Jesus. Don't you want to work normal hours? How long have you been on nights?"

"Five years, something like that and no, not really, I want to be as detached as possible." I would lose my mind if I had to deal with customers every day. I've seen them; people get stupid when they shop for food. There is nothing outside of a supermarket.

"Well, whatever, each to their own I guess." Mike says and shakes his wrist until his executive watch slides out from under his cuff. "That's nearly four hours. Quick Jane just messaged me saying we can go over. You up for a sniff?"

"It's Tuesday.

"I know."

18

"Sure, why not?"

We've been buying drugs off Quick Jane since college; everybody buys drugs from Quick Jane. She was maybe nearly fifty and served anything you like straight out of her front room whilst her old man belched and farted and watched shitty TV right there next to you. These days I generally only buy something to chill me out every couple of weeks or so. Recently Mike's been buying the higher end products. The perks of a pay cheque that is substantially more than toilet paper.

After we finish our drinks we go out to Mike's car, lighting up cigarettes as we get in.

"Won't Helen be pissed at you?"

"Helen's always pissed at me. Don't get married." He says as he twists the ignition and angles us out of the car park and onto the road. We're at the fat end of dusk now and everything is dark and damp and miserable.

Mike pulls up across the street from Quick Jane's and kills the engine. We get out under flickering streetlights and cross the road.

Quick Jane's front yard is a desolate splat of concrete with a tangle of kid's bikes growing like weeds out of a crack. Mike raps his knuckles on the front door and we wait. Eventually somebody's distorted silhouette appears the other side of the frosted glass and Jane's husband opens the door.

"Yeah?" Wally says. He is a fat man wearing the same jeans and vest and dressing gown combination as always.

"Hey Wally, how's it going? Jane said it was cool to come over."

"Did she now?"

"Yeah."

"Come in then." Wally waves us in half-heartedly and shuts the door behind us.

In the living room Jane is sitting on the saggy couch weighing out gram bags of weed. A couple of her kids are building towers out of blocks, another couple are colouring in pictures in books. Wally settles back down in his chair. I don't even know how many kids Jane has.

"Hello boys." Jane says without looking up.

"How's it going Jane?" Mike asks, rubbing his hands together. One of the soaps is on the television. Wally likes to watch the soaps.

"It's going the same as ever. This place is like a supermarket" She says running her thumb and forefinger over the seal of the last baggy and tossing it in a shoebox. She looks up. "What do you want?" Everything is straight to the point with Quick Jane; I guess that's how she got her name.

"Two white, two green." Mike says it like he's said it a thousand times before.

"And you?"

"Just one green." I say and Jane nods and pushes the shoebox to our side of the coffee table. "Help yourself." I pick out a bag and replace it with a ten. Mike takes two and puts in twenty.

"Timmy." Jane says to the kid that's just knocked over a tower. Timmy doesn't reply or even show that he's heard. "Timmy." She says louder and Timmy looks up. "Go and get me the SpongeBob DVD.

"I don't know where it is." Timmy says restacking the blocks that have fallen around him.

"It's on the shelf in the other room. Where it always is."

"Oh. Okay." He says standing and hitching his trousers up with his thumbs and he walks out of the room.

"Fucking kid." Jane says shaking her head. Mike counts out another five twenty pound notes.

We pull up outside Megamarket at ten past twelve. I'm buzzed up and not bothered about being late. Mike passes me the baggy and I take a final bump off my door key.

"Thanks man." I say rubbing crumbs of coke out of my nostrils. "How do I look?" And I tilt my face up towards Mike who is drumming his hands on the wheel to the beat of the music that only he can hear.

"You're all good buddy." He says and laughs, "You're going to have a good night."

This is your life and it's ending one shift at a time.

Three fifteen and I'm alone in the canteen wearing sunglasses anyway to hide my hollowed out eyes. This is the post buzz. Twenty-four-hour news with the sound up but low and no remote to shut it off.

Jesus Christ.

My mouth is like a beach and I'm dizzy as Politicians and community leaders mime outrage at the latest whatever it is. Samuel is down there looking for me, casing me all night for being late. Samuel enjoys your sweating apologies but that won't be the end of it. A nightshift is bad enough; a nightshift on a comedown is almost unbearable. My eyes raw and heavy behind the dark glasses, my feet twitching to the beat of some unheard music at the end of deadweight legs.

"You're supposed to tell me before you go for your break?" Samuel is at my throat.

"Jesus Christ, where did you come from?"

"Why are you wearing sunglasses?"

"Migraine." I say and watch his eyes narrow with suspicion. "It just came on all of a sudden. Bright lights. Eyes. The lights." I'm not even listening to myself. Samuel straightens up and looks down at me. "My office; ten minutes."

"Okay Samuel." I say and he turns on his heels and walks out.

Fucker doesn't even have an office.

Inside the manager's office Samuel tells me to take a seat. I take the managers seat, the swivel one. Samuel tells me to take a different seat. He takes the managers seat whilst the managers framed family looks on. I sit in the chair furthest from the manager's desk, nearest the door. Samuel tells me to stop dicking around and take the sunglasses off.

Sitting down in a sensible non-dicking around chair I peel the Wayfarers off my face. The baggy of weed in my sock rubbing against my ankle.

"Jesus Christ." Samuel looks honest to God disturbed. He pushes his glasses up his nose and I say, "It's a pretty bad migraine, Sam. Samuel. Samuels." I wonder if I'm slurring. It's hard to tell.

"Look," he says, "we both know that you're not having a migraine."

CHAPTER FOUR

I don't even bother waiting for the bus.

There's nothing in town but a crush but I'm tired and everything seems muted. A dense mud of people shoving and pushing along their individual streams. Every second is important in the race for work. I try and rub it all out of my eyes but they keep coming. Somebody is sitting in the doorway of The Crown, just looking at the morning rush by, a loose knot of blankets over his legs. I stagger over and sit down heavily next to him.

"Morning." He says. I look at him and nod. He's wearing a beaten up black suit and a black tie is knotted formally at his throat. When you're watching the rush hour at thigh level it's like watching some massive, living jungle. I sit quietly and try to centre myself.

"Do you smoke?" I say eventually, pulling out my cigarettes and offering them to him.

"I smoked for forty years and then I stopped for twenty three years and then I started again last week." He tells me and pinches a cigarette between his bony fingers. "Thank you very much." He purses it between his thin lips, patches of beard sprouting around his mouth. I notice how happy he looks.

"You're dressed smart for sleeping in a doorway." I say to him and he laughs, the cigarette wobbling between his gums. I pass him my lighter.

"My wife died about a month ago. I'm still in mourning."

"Sorry to hear that." I say and we sit quietly for a few moments before I say, "You don't come across many married folk who sleep in doorways."

"It's how I like it." He says smoking happily.

"Did your wife like it?" I say and suddenly he's looking at me sharply.

"We lived in a house, we had a home together. Not real without her though. It didn't feel *authentic*."

"So you chose what? To live on the streets?"

"I prefer the term transient. I chose to live in a more transient way." He says and I wonder what he's been on. "When Alice died I lost my anchor. And everything else just kind of swirled away."

"I'm sure there are people that can help you. Like the council or someone. Doctors maybe?"

"You don't understand. I don't want help, I have money. I chose to uncouple myself from consequence. I chose to be free." He crushes the cigarette out against the wall next to him and gathers up his blankets. He is not wearing any shoes or socks. "I chose to become a consequence man and I've never been happier."

I don't know what to say so I don't say anything and just look at him dumbly. He sees my face getting the puzzled furrows and laughs again. His hand in his pocket rummaging pulls out a folded up square of black paper. "Here," He says handing it over to me. "Look at this."

The square of paper in my hand says very simply in white capped letters.

COLBY STEIN. CONSEQUENCE MAN. HOPE PLAZA HOTEL

It was dated this coming Saturday.

"What is this?" I ask.

"This is an invitation to change your life."

"My whole life?"

"Hell, the whole damn world." He whistles. "Yes, son; that is your invitation right there." He begins to pack his blankets away into plastic carrier bags. "Anyway, I have to be going. Thanks for the smoke."

And just like that he merges with the crowd and he's gone. Bare feet and all.

At home I put the black flier on the table along with the notice of disciplinary procedure signed by the great Samuel Walters. I pull the weed out of my sock and roll a joint. For a while I stare vacantly at the switched off television and sit thinking about homeless old men with no shoes who have themselves chosen to jump off the ladder.

I am Stacker and it is a fact that working nights is bad for the skin. The lack of vitamin D and fresh air has the effect of turning you waxy and translucent. I can almost see through my own hand these days. I haven't eaten a vegetable in months.

I am a product of my environment.

Working nights is bad for your health. Your average human being is designed to do things during the days and sleep at night. This is worth a fifty pence premium.

Megamarket is so wide that it looks short. Butted up against the night, dappled streetlight orange but its glass frontage permanently lit up inside by hundreds of clinical strip lights. A beehive of twenty-four seven repetitions.

Working graveyard means we have to go through the yard to get inside. An on time bus means I'm early so I stop for a smoke before I go in. Skin Tom is already out here. We say good evenings and I sit down next to him and we sit there staring at the brick wall in front of us.

"I need a new job." He says, "Or a new life."

"No you don't, we're living the dream right here." I say through the smoke.

"Doesn't it drag you down?" He asks. "Why aren't you doing anything with your degree?"

"Sure it drags me down but whatever I did would drag me down."

"You could do some graduate scheme or something; earn some decent money at least." He says and throws the butt of his cigarette into the bucket where it hisses against the scummy water. He lights another one.

"I just don't really want to get too involved, you know? I don't want to over commit. This is as close as you can get to dropping out totally without signing on and that suits me fine."

"One day we're going to die though and we'll get replaced by robots or trained monkeys. Makes me feel shitty when I think about it too much." Workers in supermarkets are surprisingly frequent existential casualties. It's the nature of the work. We sit there silently, I can't think of any words of comfort. My own ongoing existential crisis doesn't allow any.

In the locker room, knotting my tie I wonder how easy it would be to train a monkey to do my job. Probably pretty easy I decide, with the right rewards and positive reinforcement. Primate Stacker. Robots would probably be cheaper in the long run though. Less shit to mop up.

At the bottom of the stairs Samuel is waiting for me, I can tell he's just been in the walk-in freezer because his glasses are steamed up and dripping.

"Evening." He says taking them off and rubbing them on his tie and squinting at me

"Evening." I say back and I can tell he's judging whether I'm pissed or stoned or what. He puts his glasses back on and smiles at me. "Zeus is sick tonight, you're down first aisle." He says and his smile widens. First aisle is the short straw; canned goods and spices; nasty, fiddly, densely packed cages filled with small packing boxes.

"Okay." I say and smile back and for a moment we just stand there looking at each other with these fake smiles stuck to our faces. He even opens the door for me. I start to walk towards the back of store warehouse when he calls me back.

"I nearly forgot," He says, "This is for you." And he hands me a plain white envelope. I know what this is straight away but he tells me anyway; "Confirmation of your disciplinary." With that shit eating grin grin and those blinking eyes.

From Thursday through to Saturday the workload of cages steeply increases. The sharp end of the week. On a fulltime contract you work one in two Saturdays. This is my weekend off. Earlier Mike text me saying; "Sunday lunch at the dog. Get all the old gang out."

In America people have underground bunkers in their yards jam packed with canned food and long life milk just in case. You don't hear of too many underground bunkers in Britain but I suppose they exist, probably in Scotland.

One of the memories I have of my father is that he wouldn't entertain the thought of baked beans on a cooked breakfast. Said it was disgusting.

Low fat beans.

Low salt beans.

Samuel has got the fear early this morning and he sends Felix down to pitch in with me. Felix is a man of about forty who used to be a woman of about thirty five. He has spiked up hair and a fat arse and speaks like a pastiche of a builder. Felix is smart though.

"In 1974, they raised a steamboat from the Missouri river," Felix tells me, "The Bertrand, which sank in 1865. They opened up a can of peaches and they did all their tests and they ate them. And you know what?"

"No, what?"

"They tasted just fine. One hundred and nine years old. Just fine." We don't talk and carry on stacking in silence for a bit.

"How do you know that?" I ask eventually, facing up the shallow cans of spaghetti hoops. If you face up as you go your life becomes marginally more bearable when you hit the hard yards.

"The internet; you can find out anything on the internet."

"But why did you want to find that out?"

"Why not? It's all on the internet." The God of the twenty first century is information, the internet is his church. Somebody told me that there is more information in a tabloid newspaper than what your average person would acquire over a lifetime one hundred years ago.

At five fifty Samuel calls us over and tells us that face up has to be 100% today because the suits are expecting a visit from the bigger suits. These visits happen every so often and get everybody all rattled and scatty. This sense of unease grows and festers and filters all the way down to Samuel who sweats and flusters even more than usual. I still don't really care.

In my pocket the confirmation of my disciplinary preliminary meeting bends and creases against my thigh. It tells me I have been *invited* to attend above stated meeting on Monday of next week at ten in the morning. Because this doesn't tie in with my contractual hours I am *invited* to work an eight till five standard shift in order that I might be in the store at the appropriate time for the above stated meeting.

"Do you like this job Felix?"

"I like it because it's quiet and nobody calls me queer."

"That's fair enough I suppose." We're halfway down the first side, moving at a slow pace, methodical in our work.

Extra sweet sweetcorn.

Super sweet sweetcorn.

A thousand cans of tuna fish

CHAPTER FIVE

The number twelve going out of town is on time and practically empty. I sit at the back and watch the town thin out into the suburbs and then into satellite villages, little nowhere places where nothing much happens. The safe middle ground.

I press the orange STOP button on the rail in front of me and we pull over at the bottom of the hill that leads to Haywoods and I get off yawning. If you finish work at seven in the morning and have something in mind to do, it is best to just carry on and do it as opposed to stopping and sleeping and then going at it.

The hill is steep and I climb it slowly and I'm out of breath when I reach the top. I think about giving up smoking and drinking and drugs. I think about living a pure and clean life while smoking a cigarette by the big stone gatepost that bears the smart bronze plaque saying HAYWOODS HOME. When I've finished I walk up the steep driveway which is at right angles to the hill I have just climbed. Either side of me are inpatient cared for foliage and young saplings planted optimistically in the spring by people who may have died before they even took root. The driveway wobbles right then left then right again before sweeping round grandly to the left where the home itself is presented. In front of it is a finely kept lawn tended to by professionals. These old and sick folk are not trusted with ride on lawnmowers and power tools.

Pressing the buzzer at the front door I wait for the receptionist to unlock it which she does with a push of a button on the counter.

"Good morning." She says.

"Hi, Sandy, how's it going?" Sandy has been sitting at the reception counter every time I have visited my father for as long as I can remember. Her ruddy face and cheerfully heaving tits are almost furniture.

"It's going good." She says smiling as I scribble my name in the visitor book. "We haven't seen you for a while."

"It's difficult with work." I say. This part of the home is closed off by another set of double doors and it smells of lavender and vanilla. They spray the plastic flowers with air freshener. "Your mum was here yesterday." Sandy says. "I think she cut his toenails."

Through the second set of doors, into the guts of the place it stinks of piss and shit and cabbage. Here they don't bother to spray the plastic flowers. My father is on the second floor, where they keep the long termers closeted away. I don't think they even have plastic flowers up there. In the corridor as I wait for the elevator I watch a procession of shuffling chronics head towards the breakfast room. An old man, skeleton thin and yellow salutes me and I nod back.

"They're trying to kill me." He gums in a thin voice. "You've got to help me."

"Don't start Patrick. Come along to breakfast." A young girl dressed in a nurse's smock comes back for him and gently guides him forward. She smiles apologetically at me and I smile back. The circle of life is completed when you're shitting yourself and treated like a child.

The elevator door groans as it opens and I step in and as the doors close behind me I find myself looking at my tired reflection. I don't look good; I look burnt out and weary. How have I got here? When did I slip? Irrelevant questions now I suppose, because here is where I am. It feels like a year has passed by the time the doors open on the second floor and sighing to myself I step out onto the low grade grey carpet. It is quiet on this floor. People up here don't talk very much. I turn left out of the elevator and follow the corridor as it dog-legs round to the right. My father is in the room at the end of the corridor. I take two deep breaths before I go in.

He lies there perfectly still, the blankets pulled up to his chest. There is a thick tube down his throat and two thinner ones in his nostrils. These tubes connect up with a big black box on the table next to him which in turn connects to a screen which displays his vitals. His eyes are closed but his eyebrows have grown out bushy and wild giving him the impression of mild surprise. His arms lay uselessly by his side and it seems that my mum may have cut his toenails but not his finger nails which are yellowed and talon-like. His hair is cut every two weeks by the in-house hairdresser and is styled in a thin and flaccid side part. I look at him sadly for a moment before sitting down in the chair to the left of the bed.

He was a Shipbroker before everything went south in the mid-nineties. He had started to drink heavily when his company lost a lot of continental work to Paris and Hamburg. He had life insurance which, so his letter went, would be substantial enough to take care of us until Robert and I matured. Unfortunately this would only pay out on receipt of a valid death certificate. His company subsidised health insurance paid out enough each month to pay for his room and care at Haywoods. The staff didn't mind because he was easy work. He didn't care because he was unable. I think deep down my mum knows she needs to let him go but there is a bitch of a difference between knowing something and acting on it. It's not something we talk about.

I visit every couple of months or so but for no other reason than it feels like what I'm supposed to do. I know it keeps mum happy but I never talk to him on these visits. I can't see the point. It doesn't make sense to me to speak to something which is little more than an object. Sometimes I wonder that if he had kept his shit together how our lives would have turned out. I always try and push these thoughts away before they get to much grip and purchase inside me.

When I was a boy we used to holiday out on the east coast every summer, with the wind pummeling in off the North Sea and the rainy day ice creams he used to say they were proper British seaside holidays. The few days when the sun shone Robert and me would kick along the beach as our parents walked the prom arm in arm.

One holiday, when I was maybe eight or nine, Robert kicked our football into the sea and it rode away atop of the waves growing smaller and smaller. My dad, he kicked off his shoes and just ran into the water, fully clothed and swam after it until he too grew smaller and smaller. And you know what? He got that damn ball back. He got that ball back and then we went and got fish and chips. I remember him queuing up to get four times cod and chips soaking wet and dripping all over. I remember my parents laughing and I remember we sat on the pier and watched the sun dip down over the sea. We were a happy family those days. I was proud.

Another time when Robert had stayed behind with mum, dad and I had gone into town to get something, I can't remember what and on the way back I got sick. Bent over double with stomach pains and my dad carried me back in his arms like I was nothing weightier than a rag doll.

I used to love those holidays. We didn't have enough.

I remember the day it happened. I was at school. I was in Mrs Fleet's class that year and she had invented this evil thing called Tuesday's Times Table Test. This always took place after lunch and I had, as was my nature back then, spent the entire lunch break worrying about it. I hadn't wanted to kick the mini football about with my friends that day and had spent the whole hour sitting on one of the swings in the playground letting my feet scuff along the rutted dirt. I remember the horrible hollow feeling of dread echo around my chest and stomach and I remember watching the birds sitting on the chain link fence around the school grounds and being jealous of them and their ability to just up and fly away from anything that bothered them or threatened their peacefulness. When the end of lunchtime bell rang I trudged back to class walking slowly and on my own with the wheels in my brain jamming themselves over the cruelty of multiplication.

I sat next to a kid called Mark Sawyer that term and God knows what happened to him but he was good at his times tables I remember that. We sat down and Mrs Fleet, her whole appearance made up out of different shades of grey, came round and handed out photocopies of the ten question test. I remember her standing up in front of the blackboard and her mouth was just opening but before she could say the word "Begin." There was a fast and urgent rapping on the classroom door and the school receptionist Miss Haylock entered and quickly walked up to Mrs Fleet and whispered something in her ear. I remember the creases in her face resetting themselves from school teacher calm into school teacher concern. She called me forward and I remember thinking that I can't be in trouble because I haven't failed the test yet and I remember seeing a bird sitting on the fence outside the classroom who seemed to be watching me with its black beady eyes. Miss Haylock led me to the school reception where she sat me down and explained that my dad had been taken into hospital and that my mum was on her way to collect me and my brother. I was told to go and get my bag and my coat and to come back here. I remember her giving me a hug and telling me to hurry and with a child's perception I could detect undercurrents of something serious in her voice.

Mum had collected Robert before me as his school was first on the route and he was sat in the front. I remember her driving towards the hospital, at a speed much quicker than she usually drove.

I remember that there was a lot of waiting around that afternoon.

Eventually we were allowed into see my dad. He was lying there in bed perfectly still, like he is today but his neck was purple and swollen and his eyes were dark and bruised.

I remember being glad to have got out of the times table test.

CHAPTER SIX

Hope Plaza and its adjacent hotel were planned and built as a symbol of optimism for the new millennium, as the feel good nineties wound down and pre-millennial tension built and every self-respecting town, city, borough and village needed to build something or plant something. It was called Hope Plaza as opposed to Millennium Plaza apparently so it became timeless.

Today even hope has become appropriated. By the fountain in the centre of the massive white marbled surface a knot of skinheads is growing by the minute. Some of them are carrying the Union flag, others the cross of George. Some are chanting defence league slogans. Somebody is standing on the raised edge of the fountain firing everyone up with a megaphone.

And still they come.

In the reception of the Hope Plaza Hotel an A-frame sign tells me that the Colby Stein, Consequence seminar begins at noon in the auditorium suite. A bent up old American lady dressed all in brown is at my elbow practically vibrating with excitement saying; "This is going to change your life."

"Is that right?" I say suddenly aware of the babble and chatter all around the hotel's reception. The old lady is clasping my arm and saying, "You need to have an open mind. Just trust me." The current of the crowd carries her away.

Looking about me I see the one still and silent entity in the place is an old man sitting in an upright wingback chair over by the rack of leaflets for local attractions. He is wearing a beige suit and sunglasses and sitting as a statue, impassive and set. In his lap is a concertinaed white cane. I wonder if Colby Stein can cure the blind. I merge with the crowd and we funnel into a corridor at the back of the reception area. Maybe ten or so people in front of me I can see Skin Tom, his thick tattooed neck and shaved scalp unmistakable. I think about calling out to him but not knowing the first thing about what a Colby Stein consequence seminar actually is and whether I want to be seen attending one, I decide against.

At the end of the corridor the double doors to the auditorium are open wide and people are sitting up and down the steep banked seats. I enter the room just in time to see Skin Tom take a seat about halfway down on the left side. I sit half a dozen rows behind him, next to a girl with half a shaved head and a many pierced face. A smartly dressed black man follows into my row and sits on my right. He nods a hello but it's nothing more than an instinctive gesture, his eyes are focussed but faraway. He gathers his trousers at the knees as he folds himself into his seat.

When the place is filled to capacity somebody shuts the door. All around me people are whispering in hissed excitable voices.

After a few minutes the lights dim down and with them so does the babble.

A single white dot appears on the large movie screen at the back of the stage and everybody focuses. The dot grows and grows and grows until it becomes clear that we are looking at an image of earth. Next the picture of our planet is replaced by a rapid tumble of images; a dense black forest yields to dinosaurs yields to Neanderthal yields to the great pyramids. Faster and faster; a tablet of ancient Greek text, Julius Caesar, the Roman army, a massive catapult firing burning rocks. Discordant droning music soundtracks the whole thing as the images shoots by in fractions of seconds. Here is an ancient King. A graveyard. A long boat. William Shakespeare, white light refracted through a prism. A fire sweeping a city. HMS Victory, a group of slaves tilling a field. Abraham Lincoln. Queen Victoria. Adolf Hitler. A million dead Jews. A nuclear mushroom cloud. A young girl burnt by napalm.

The fall of the Berlin wall. Princess Diana.

The World Trade Centre. Osama Bin Laden.

Nelson Mandela.

A burning dollar bill.

A question mark.

The jangle of music reaches its climax and the screen smashes to black and we're back in dark silence. A single bright spotlight snaps on lighting up the middle of the stage. There is a sharp collective inhale of breath. You can smell the anticipation.

Somebody walks out across the stage and into the light and everybody stands up and applauds, some people scream, some people whistle and Colby Stein, standing in his pillar of light accepts it all. He is a tall man, dressed completely in black and he looks out at us with his hands mated behind his bald head. After a minute or so he holds up his hands and slowly lowers them to his side. The applause dies down and people retake their seats. The girl next to me is sweaty and giddy and grinning happily.

"Good afternoon, first of all I'd like to thank you all for coming today." His voice is quiet even through the microphone clipped onto his shirt. "I'm sure many of you are unsure of what to expect, what is a consequence man? Who am I? What am I going to talk to you about? Well, first of all, as you know, this seminar is completely free. My group pays for the venue and I talk to you not for profit but because I want to help you. My group and I engage in fundraising activities all year round and this enables us to hold these seminars at no cost to you. At the end of the seminar, hopefully some of you will be inspired enough to sign up and join us, maybe some of you will even want to donate. If you do, that's great. If you don't that is also fine. There is no pressure."

The guy next to me has taken a small pad of paper and a pen from his pocket and is taking fast, scrappy notes.

"The definition of consequence is the result or outcome of something that has occurred at an earlier time. If you throw a ball into the air it will fall back down. This is the result of gravity. This is a consequence. Some consequences, like the ones written into the laws of physics are irrefutable. These are factual consequences and there is nothing that can be done to change them. In a million years, if somebody throws a ball into the air it will still fall back down to earth. Nothing to be done about these." He begins to move around the stage, the spotlight moving with him.

"Now, the other types of consequences are the manmade ones. The laws and the rules that govern us and keep us in check through fear of the consequences of breaking them. This fear is instilled in us from the first moments that we are able to think for ourselves and we are taught. No, we are *conditioned* into accepting, without questioning this all-encompassing matrix of rules and regulations which are designed, so we are told, for our own good. Now, it used to be that nobody questioned anything. Sure, you had your alternative groups; the hippies, the activists, the communists, the punks who stood up and called out for a different way but the changes that they advocated were still enclosed within the existing framework designed by the men in the towers. People whose lives do not resemble the experience of the everyday man and woman." He pauses and smiles out at his audience.

"Does anybody remember the sixties?" He asks and a handful of people raise their arms. "It was a good time. The Beatles, The Stones, Bob Dylan, some of the greatest musicians that the world has ever seen. Free love, flower power, the advent of civil rights. All these things and a million more all came about because it was a time of hope. The Second World War was like a bad dream. They were living in the future then. They were living in hope. There was a feeling that anything was possible that the will of the people would triumph over whatever adversity came its way. But the sixties failed. Ultimately they failed because the men in the suits who drive the machine knew exactly which buttons to press. The myth of people having any kind of genuine power was exposed and after that brief and precious supernova of love and laughter and free will the status quo was soon resumed.

These days there are still protests about unjust wars, about unjust capitalist balance, about unjust Politicians. But these make absolutely no difference to anything. They are all just background noise. The wheels keep on turning as fast as they ever have even in the face of catastrophic financial meltdown. Nothing ever changes. We need to think again. We need to empower ourselves to act authentically within ourselves without the fear of consequence. Because it is that fear which has kept you impotent for all of your life and it will continue to do so unless you own it."

For two and a half hours Colby Stein spoke, his voice sometimes soft and comforting sometimes powerful and strident but all the time persuading and cajoling. Back in the reception area and the wingback chair is empty the blind old man nowhere to be seen. People are spilling out of the auditorium and nobody looks like they know what to make of what we have just seen. Outside the Skinhead demonstration has swollen and taken over the whole of Hope Plaza, they're chanting and singing and you can see them jumping around in the fountain through the windows and the Hotel's front doors.

Almost on auto-pilot I head towards the bar and order a pint of something strong and bland. There must be a good two or three thousand out there, all of them looking the same with their shaved heads and bulldog tattoos and too tight T-shirts. They all sound pissed up and angry. Parked up at the side of the Plaza I can see a television news camera van. This is what it means to be British in the bloody abortion that is the twenty first century so far. Fascism and reality TV. The dumber you are the louder you are the more people listen. I neck half the pint and shake my head at the whole fucking mess of it all.

Out of nowhere a chair is thrown from the doors of the Hotel into the skinheads and for a moment everybody stops and the world is quiet and still. And then as if as one entity everybody turns in the direction of the Hotel and somebody throws a bottle and the scene explodes into a surge of violence and through the window of the bar I can see people of all ages and descriptions spilling out of the Hotel swinging balled fists and chairs. A fat skinhead with tattooed tears on his cheeks cracks some kid in the jaw and the kid drops. Mayhem and carnage and bruises and blood. The receptionist runs into the bar and grabs the phone off the wall and punches in 999 and says "We need the Police at the Hotel Plaza." And then, "A lot of them." It's like a war outside and I sit and watch it with an anesthetising sense of removed alarm, like I'm watching a television screen.

I'm aware of movement at my side and I look around and I'm both surprised and totally unsurprised to see Colby Stein leaning on the bar next to me watching the violence with a serene sense of detachment. He nods at me and says, "If you remove the consequence people will do things that they never thought possible." A bottle crashes against the window leaving a jagged crack and somebody screams. The barman is nowhere to be seen, as likely to be fighting as he is hiding and Colby Stein sighs quietly to himself and walks around the other side of the bar and pours himself a pint.

"Do you want anything?"

"Sorry?"

"Do you want anything to drink?"

"No." I say and then. "Does this sort of thing happen a lot?" And Colby Stein shrugs as he flips off the tap and places his drink on the bar. He comes back around sucking beer off of his fingers and sits down next to me.

43

"People react differently. There's not usually a… what do you call them? Defence League? There's not usually a Defence League protest going on." He shrugs again. "People react differently." Outside sirens cut through the overcast sky but still people swing punches and launch bottles and somebody wearing a mask of blood appears at the window with somebody else grabbing at his collar. Colby Stein watches this all unflinchingly, barely interested, sipping at his beer.

"So what's your story?" He asks as calm as if nothing out of the usual is going on.

"What do you mean?" Sirens getting closer now.

"What do you do? Why are you here? It's just talking man, relax."

"I work at Megamarket. Somebody without any shoes gave me a flier. Told me it would change my life."

"Ah." Colby Stein smiles at something that I don't understand. "And has it?"

"It's too early to tell."

"You work at Megamarket?"

"Yeah."

"How is that?"

"It pays the bills. Mostly."

"You want to hear a joke?"

"Sure." I finish my beer and look around for the barman. Outside somebody has set a car on fire but people are easing up on each other now.

"I went to the doctor and told him I was feeling nihilistic. He said nothing's wrong with you." He snaps out a short sharp laugh and I nod and smile. He looks at me his dark eyes almost looking through me. "I'm going to give you my phone number. You should come and see us one time. See if we can't sort you out a better way through your life."

"What makes you think I need a better way through my life?"

"I used to work for Megamarket, I know the gig."

"Oh yeah?"

"That's right." Colby Stein finishes his drink and wipes his mouth with a paper napkin. "Now if you'll excuse me I'm going to get out of here." He pulls a pen out of his jacket pocket and writes a phone number down on a beermat. "Here you go." He says. "You should give us a call."

CHAPTER SEVEN

I arrive at The Dog at the same time as Owen and we say hellos to each other and stand under the canopy smoking cigarettes. Owen and I have known each other since college which is really when we all started hanging out together. Owen was smart and driven and knew that he wanted to be an accountant since he was a kid. That's what his old man did and his old man before him. Owen's ambition was a house and a wife and a kid or two. Kind of straight edged but not to the extent of being defined by it.

"You're looking well, mate." Owen always says this to whoever he's talking to, it's like his stock opening gambit. In my case I know it's not true but I say. "Thanks, man. How are you keeping?"

"Oh, you know how it goes."

"Sure."

"Keeping busy, keeping busy. You know how it goes." Owen smokes menthol cigarettes but only when his wife and kid weren't around and he stabs it out in a Carlsberg ashtray.

"Sam not about?" I ask jetting blue smoke out of my nostrils.

"Nah, she's taken Bobby to her parents for the weekend."

"Cool." I say trashing my cigarette in the tray and opening the door for us. We walk in and up to the bar and take a couple of free stools. The Dog always gets busy for Sunday lunch. It was on the edge of town, not a million miles away from Megamarket, where the town trickles out into the suburbs and little clusters of villages that settled around its periphery.

Somebody whistles from behind us and we turn around. Mike and Helen wave at us from a corner table.

"When are you going to settle down?" Owen asks me as we wait for a barman to come over.

"Oh. I don't know if that's for me."

"Sure it is. You just need to find the right girl." People think that you're lacking something important if you burn out the last days of your twenties without a significant other. Maybe they're right.

"Still at Megamarket?"

"Yeah."

"Still on nights?"

"Yeah." A barman comes over and takes our order. It's been less than a month since I last saw Owen but he likes to make sure he's up to date. To Owen, apathy is not reading the share prices. I can't relate to that degree of interest in anything. I'm thinking about what Colby Stein said. I'm thinking about violence. Owen wants the whole world to settle down.

We take our drinks over to where Mike and Helen are sitting and everybody says hello all over again.

"Lucy is coming." Helen says and elbows me in the ribs.

"Fantastic." I say and immediately feel like walking out.

"Is that alright?" Mike asks, detecting the flatness in my voice. "You guys are cool aren't you?" As far as the world is concerned everything is cool. I mean we've seen each other since the big break up and nothing much happened.

Everything is cool.

"Sure." I say and think about climbing into my pint glass. I take a long sip instead.

"So…" Owen says, "What's new with you guys? You're looking well."

"Nothing much." Mike says rubbing his nose and looking at Helen. Mike's a bit like me in as much as he finds the concept of adult life just outside his field of comprehension; he just wants to talk about football and betting. That's where we differ. I don't want to talk about anything.

"Well, we're redecorating the dining room." Helen says stirring her Tonic water or whatever with her straw. The door swings open and I look up and catch myself holding my breath in nervous anticipation. Just some elderly couple walking in, arm in bony arm. I take another drink and try to relax.

"Well, I say we. What I mean is we're getting somebody in. That Dellar and Son from round the corner. My parents used them last spring, they're meant to be pretty good. Tidy workers apparently." I can see Mike fading out fast.

"I keep telling Sam that we should redo the en suite." Owen says.

"She doesn't want to?"

"She says we can't afford it."

The door opens again and this time Lucy walks in. Lucy and some guy I've never seen before.

"Oh shit." Mike says quietly. I don't say anything. Lucy and the new guy go up to the bar and sit in the seats that Owen and I sat in when we ordered our beers. Lucy turns around and her face catches the light making her look all angelic and lovely. She smiles and mouths a hello at Helen and does one of those girly waves, all smiles and hands and then she sees me and the smile abruptly dims into one of those thin sad grimaces you make at people you don't want to see. I do the same and give a short nod. Mike starts rubbing at his nose again until Helen bats his hand away and says, "You're worse than a child." Mike leans over to her and says loud enough for me to hear; "Who's the dude?"

"I don't know." Helen says and I can see her mouth purse up in confusion and then drop into a perfect red "Oh." She looks over at me and her eyes look at me with stabbing pity and I wave it away.

"It's fine." I say.

"Really?"

"Really."

Owen laughs awkwardly as Lucy and the new guy come over, drinks in hands and smiles on faces. I look into my pint glass and again wonder if I can climb in and disappear. I'm staring at it trying to remove myself from the scene. In the end I give up and neck the rest of it.

Lucy says; "Everyone, this is Christopher. We have Algebra together."

"You're looking well." Owen says shuffling around the table so Lucy and the new guy can join the group. I don't feel like calling him Christopher just yet.

"Christopher, this is everyone." Everybody says alright or hello or hiya and fucking Christopher smiles like a movie star. I stand up.

"Drink anybody?"

"Yeah man, I'll come with you. Babe?" Mike says standing up and spinning the dregs.

"Another Slim Line please." Helen answers as she chews the end of the straw.

"I'm good for now." Owen still has three quarters of a pint in front of him. Mike and I quit the table for the bar.

I throw a twenty onto a beer towel and stumble fall onto the bar stool. Mike sits down next to me.

"You cool, man?"

"Yeah."

"Yeah?"

"I mean what the fuck?" I say quietly, almost sadly. It had been a bad breakup. Three years' worth of pretending and avoiding all blown up in spectacular and brutal fashion by yours truly. It's fair to say that there were regrets.

"It's been a good couple of months, man."

"I know how long it's been."

"They could be just friends." Mike picks up my twenty and folds it and puts it into my shirt pocket. "I'll get these." He says.

"Fancy a Tequila?" I ask him the idea all of a sudden luminous in front of me.

"It's Sunday lunch..."

"Yeah, so?"

"Okay. Make sure Helen doesn't see." Mike says as he catches the barman's eye and nods him over. I glance back at the happy campers; nobody even knows we exist at this point in time. Everybody is laughing.

The barman lines up two shots and two fat slices of lemon in front of two fresh pints and hands Mike his change saying "Enjoy."

We knock them back at duck our heads low down to suck the lemon and in the back of my head synapses explode and crackle to life.

"Fucking Mexicans, man." Mike says shaking his head and slurping the foam off his pint. "They know how to drink." I slap him on the back encouragingly and we stand up and head back to the table the first hint of a blur behind my eyes, that here we go again feeling in my stomach and in my knees.

Sitting back down Helen says, "You forgot my drink."

"Fuck me." Mike says immediately standing up again. "Back in a minute." He goes back to the bar to try again.

"How are you doing?" Lucy asks, looking at me with those big dark eyes with her fingers tapping the base of her wine glass.

"I'm doing good." I say and try to think of something else to say.

"How's your mum?" Tapping away nervously.

"She's alright." I say. "Same old mum."
Owen is talking to Christopher about something and Lucy tilts her head to listen and then laughs.

"He's such a funny kid." She says and takes a delicate sip of Chardonnay.

"I've got a sister his age." Christopher says, "Step sister actually. Kids are hilarious at that age." Christopher speaks in a neat, well-bred voice. Mike is rubbing his nose again.

"What is up with you?" Helen asks sharply.

"Nothing." Mike sniffs. "I've got an itchy nose, that's all."

"How's Uni?" Helen asks Lucy closing her shoulder on Mike.

"It's getting difficult now." Lucy says. Lucy is in the second year of her Maths Masters at the University. Lucy is goal orientated.

"Second year is tough." Christopher says as if somebody had asked him.

"Where are you from Chris?" Mike asks placing Helen's drink in front her.

"Christopher." He says. "I'm from West London. Twickenham."

"Nice part of the world."

Their wedding flashes into my field of vision. Everybody neat and clipped and smart and happy. Their house in the suburbs. Their picture book kids. Mr and Mrs whatever living happily ever after whilst I stack the shelves for them.

"I'm going for a cigarette." I say and stand up on jelly jointed legs.

"I keep telling Luce to give it up." Christopher says shaking his head.

"Yeah, good luck with that." I say and walk away.

Outside I sit on the table of the bench and light a cigarette, the wind whips up sharply against my face and the clouds above bloom into dark grey mountains of untold heights and everything feels apocalyptic.

The door swings open and I'm surprised to be unsurprised that it's Lucy. She pulls her silk scarf up around her throat. She looks at me and I look at her and she gives another thin smile only this time it's somewhat warmer and sadder.

"Hey." She says quietly.

"Hey, yourself." I say back. She drops her bag onto the bench and rummages inside and pulls out a pack of Lights.

"Can I use your lighter?" She asks as if everything is totally normal and fine.

"Sure." I pass it to her and she lights up and passes it back.

"Are you okay?"

"He seems nice." I say flatly and look away towards the apocalypse.

"We're just friends." She says. "He's in my Algebra class."

Fucking Algebra.

Freshly dead leaves scurry down the street in front of us. Tumbling over each other, on the run from something that we can't see.

"Are you okay?" She asks again her cigarette smouldering untouched. "You don't seem yourself."

"I'm fine." I say but I'm thinking that I'm not sure what myself feels like anymore. All I do is stack the shelves at Megamarket and drink cheap wine. Is that really all I am these days? Looking inside myself is like falling into a black hole. The void, gaping and huge and immediate. I can almost feel myself falling through. From this close I can't see any alternatives.

I am Stacker and this is all I am. There is no redemption in a Sunday lunch with the old gang.

"I'm fine." I say again, quieter now. The leaves are picking up speed. The clouds are getting fat.

CHAPTER EIGHT

Statistically speaking if you are going to kill yourself the chances are you'll do it on a Monday. This is called the blue Monday phenomenon; it was big in the eighties. My father picked Tuesday and I think that is where he went wrong. Today isn't as bad as all that though, it's more of a brown Monday. In the fun factory with ten thousand draggy customers; Monday morning unshaved and hung over. This is why I work nights. Still disciplinary meetings being what they are you can't expect a Suit to spend half a night here just to whip my balls.

I am Stacker and I do as I'm told.

Different game during the day, you get real managers, real Suits. Everybody knows my card has got a big fat Donny Brinklow stamp on it today so everyone is being extra nice. Dead man stacking. I should have shaved though. Brinklow is big on that, likes his drones to look shiny.

Why would anybody go shopping first thing on a Monday? Do these people not have hangovers to snuggle up with? Do they not have jobs?

Brinklow calls me up to his office for our ten o clock meeting. I don't mess about with the seating. Samuel Walters' statement is lined up square on the desk. I sit here thinking that there are over a million people working in supermarkets and we should take a march. Or bomb something. Brinklow says; "I have here a statement of incident written up by your team leader Samuel Walters and he alleges that on Wednesday morning you told him to 'go and fuck yourself with a fat one you massive fascist cunt." He pauses for affect as if it needed to sink in. "What have you got to say about that?"

"Yes, that sounds about right."

"Sounds about right?" Eyebrows raised and pupils narrowed.

"Yeah, it sounds about right. It was something along those lines."

"And do you think that this is an acceptable way to speak to any member of staff here? Let alone your team leader?"

"No. Of course I don't." Deep breaths and fix eye contact. "I was having a migraine and he just wouldn't step off. I'm sorry I reacted but the guys a…"

"You don't like doing yourself favours, do you?" And he begins to shuffle a bunch of blank pages and licks his lips and nests his fingers looking at me all serious. "He says you were drunk or on drugs. Is that true?"

"Absolutely not." And Donny Brinklow lets out a big pissed off sigh as if this little pow-wow isn't the most fun he's going to have all day and he says; "Well I'm going to have to investigate this further I'm afraid."

"Why? I told you; I admit it. I called him a fascist cunt. I'm not seeing what you need to be investigating here?"

"Protocol and chain of command are what keeps us ahead of the crowd. It's what defines us."

I'm thinking written warning here, maybe final. Donny Brinklow looks back over the scribbled notes that he has taken and finally says. "You're going to be suspended for the rest of the week whilst I investigate the matter further and decide upon what course of action is appropriate here."

"Will that be paid?" I ask and Brinklow arches an eyebrow and looks at me.

CHAPTER NINE

The voice at the end of the phone says, "Get the train to Lynn, someone will pick you up at half three."

"Okay." I say and the line goes dead. What else am I going to do during paid suspension?

I pack a bag with T shirts and underwear and a cheap bottle of red for the journey and leave the flat. The day is mild and I chain smoke my way to the station.

Sitting on the platform waiting for the thirteen thirty and drinking wine and I'm starting to wonder what I'm doing. I have, I realise, no idea of where I'm going and what I'm going to find when I get there. But if they don't want me to be working during their investigations then a leap into the unknown has more potential than masturbating the week away. The question remains though, potential for what? I light a cigarette and think about what Colby Stein might have going on in the middle of nowhere. A rat faced little cleaning man wearing a high-vis jacket and trousers appears out of nowhere with a sack of trash slung over his fluorescent shoulder and says, "You can't smoke here. Can't you read?" And he points to the sign above the bench that I'm sitting on.

"Why not?" I say, "I'm outside; I'm about a hundred feet from anybody else, what's the harm? I mean, seriously?"

"Railway regulations." He says clearly getting his kicks. "Put it out or I'll call the Police." He smirks which pisses me off. I take one more big drag and blow smoke at him as I crush it out under my heel. He shakes his head but still smirks like he's won something and then he carries on picking up litter with the claw on a stick thing. When he's got to the end of the platform he loops around the last light pole and comes back. Once he's gone back passed me I light another cigarette and take another drink of wine.

Eventually the thirteen thirty rolls up and about a thousand business men in identical suits step off.

I sit down in an almost empty carriage and put my feet up and try to get comfortable. The train picks up speed and it bumps along the rails with its clunking rhythm reverberating through the floor and upholstery. Outside the world slips by in different shades of fields and ditches and the occasional spattering of farm buildings. Above it all, big rolls of dark clouds push against each other until their seams tear and thin sheets of rain spit down the windows pushed back by the wind resistance into irregular rivulets and streams.

Looking around the carriage I'm mildly alarmed to see that every other passenger is reading the Daily Flail. The same hysterical headline screaming at me in multiples. The most popular newspaper in this ridiculous island country is the one that used to sympathise with the Nazis. I can see these people as they dip their papers down and push the outer pages together in order to move through the paper and I can see them eyeing me, disgusted by my feet up and red wine stained teeth grinning at them.

Every now and then the train slows and stops in some small nowhere town station and a couple of people get off and a couple of others get on. Nobody wants to sit near me.

At Downham Market the old boy in the set of seats across from me stands up to quit the carriage, folds his paper and tosses it onto his seat and looks over at me and says, "It's wasters like you that are going to ruin this country."

I laugh and raise the bottle of wine in a toast to him. He gets off the train shaking his head and saying something about labour camps and teaching discipline.

By the time the train pulls up to Lynn the bottle is empty and I'm feeling relaxed. It's raining harder here and all about me people are scurrying about heading for taxis or any shelter they can find. I sit on my bag on the steps of the station and watch them sadly amused by the insignificance of it all.

At exactly three thirty a black Range Rover with smoked out windows pulls into the car park and somehow I just know that this is my ride. Standing up I sling my bag over my shoulder and walk over to where it is idling and straddling two disabled spaces. The front passenger window rolls down and a girl of about maybe twenty looks out at me dripping and grinning in the rain. "I assume you're the guy who called Colby?" She says.

"What gave it away?"

"It's always the weird ones." She says, "Get in the back." And her window whirs back up and I open the door behind her. Climbing in I drop my bag at my feet. There's a well-built tank of a man sitting behind the driver's side wearing a vest top which shows off his tattooed biceps, he has a don't fuck with me face and both his ears are pierced. I nod at him but he just glares at me and passes me a black bandanna folded up into the shape of a blindfold. The driver is a thin man wearing glasses who doesn't even acknowledge me.

"Put that on." The guy next to me says.

"You want to blindfold me? What the fuck?"

"No, we want you to blindfold yourself. If I was going to do it, it would be round your neck." And I'm thinking what is going on here and maybe this wasn't such a great idea after all. The girl in the front leans around and says, "It's just a precaution, that's all. No need to get uptight."

"I've just met you people." I say, "This is fucked up. There is definitely a need to get uptight."

"And we've just met you. Like I said it's just a precaution. Either you put the blindfold on or you get out of the car." She smiles and she looks damn pretty. I shrug and say, "Okay then." And I press the bandanna over my eyes and tie it at the back of my head.

"Good." Says the girl in front of me and I can feel her seat pushing against my knees as she twists back around and then I hear the driver find first gear and we begin to move. I'm feeling tense and wishing that I hadn't drunk so much wine, if I knew this was going to be some kidnapping type deal I'm not sure I would have come along. Better than being bored I suppose. I think about asking some of the questions which are stacking up in my brain but these characters don't seem like they are the sort that go in for too much sharing.

We drive in silence.

When I was seven years old I fell out of a tree and into a rosebush and the thorns scratched both of my corneas. I remember my parents rushing me to the hospital with blood trickling out of a thousand little cuts all over my face and body. The doctors doused my eyes with this special disinfectant and I had to have them tightly bandaged for two weeks as they healed. I am reminded of this as I'm driven along, blind and disorientated. I can feel it when we slow to a stop at what I assume to be traffic lights. I can sense the camber of the road as we sweep round unseen bends. I can feel the engine strain and then relax as the driver works the stick shift. I can smell the disinfectant that they sprayed on my eyes.

Being unsighted it is easy to lose track of time but I would guess we've been driving for half an hour, maybe forty minutes when we stop and the front passenger door opens as the engine idles. I can hear some sort of scraping coming from in front of the car, like maybe a gate opening and then the car creeps forward and then stops again. Maybe half a minute later the seat in front of me re-settles against my knees and the door shuts. We drive on but now I can tell that we're off road and on some sort of ill kept track with the suspension absorbing potholes and ruts. We carry on in this way for maybe another ten minutes and then we stop and the engine is killed.

"Okay." The girl says, "You can take it off now."

There is mud everywhere. I'm in a farmyard. The Range Rover is parked up untidily amongst a fist of other vehicles. There is a low slung beat up farmhouse in front of me. The girl and the driver and the tank from the backseat are walking towards the front door, I'm not moving with the bandanna wrapped around my right fist like a boxer's mitt.

"Gonna stand out in the rain all afternoon?" The girl calls back over her shoulder. The driver has already opened the door and disappeared inside, I get the impression that he's a bit of a dick. The tank shrugs behind the girl but has lost his tense menace now we're all out of the car and back to what I assume to be sanctuary.

Inside we're in the kitchen, a big room with a rugged big table at its core. The Tank pushes the door closed behind me. On the table are old newspapers and stacks of heavy looking books. The girl smiles warmly and says, "Hi I'm Zara." And she holds out her hand. "Who are you?" After a pause I say, "I'm Stacker."

"And you wonder why we wanted you blindfolded." She giggles in the way that pretty girls do. "This is Joey. He looks like a jerk but he's alright really." Joey nods and says, "Hey man."

"The guy who was driving is Ewan, he is a jerk." Zara says walking over to the full length fridge and opening the door. "Anybody want a beer?"

"I'll go for one of those." Joey says lean sitting against the table. Zara looks at me with her eyebrows. "Sure," I say, "I'll take a beer, thanks."

"Okay then, good start." She says and takes out three cold misted bottles. She begins opening and closing draws along the length of the counter. "I can never remember where we keep the-" She pulls out a small metal opener and pops the tops and spaces them between us on the table. "Sit down, if you like?" She says and sits down herself. Joey stays in his lean.

Footsteps in the hallway and looking up to the doorway I see the homeless guy from The Crown come into the kitchen still in his suit and still without shoes. The worn out tapestry look of his sprouts of beard from before are now thickened into a good weeks growth. He laughs when he sees me sitting at the table and says, "Didn't I tell you, you'd change your life?"

"I'm not sure anything has changed just yet, not dramatically anyway."

"It will son, it will. Give it time. It will." He walks over to the fridge and says, "Well if everybody else is." And picks himself a beer. He goes straight to the right draw and cracks his open. "Ewan went straight up to Colby, I see him go by when I was dozing in there."

"This is Stacker."

"Well that's a fucking stupid name, if I may say." Says Bare Feet, "My name is Johnny Wriggles." He sits down next to Zara and takes out a pouch of tobacco from his shirt pocket. He pulls out a cigarette paper and begins rolling a knuckle of it into a tube. When he's done, he licks the gum and rolls it across the table to me. "I owe you one." And I'm thinking what is this; the fucking Walton's or something? And then Ewan walks back in and I see for the first time how thin and pale his face is like a skinny Joseph Goebbels. Now, rolling himself a cigarette Johnny Wriggles raises his voice to Ewan who is walking behind him back to the door we came in through. "Well, did you wake him up?"

"Yeah, he's awake." Ewan says and opens the door, "I'm going to check the traps; you all make yourself all nice and cosy." He pulls the door shut behind him not hard enough to be a slam but not soft enough to be misunderstood.

"What traps is he going to check?" I say, thinking more Manson family than Walton's. "There's a lake across the south field, we set traps for geese." Zara says and I say, "Oh." Johnny strikes a match and cups it to his mouth and then tosses the box to me and I do the same.

"Colby will be down soon." Zara explains, "He likes to nap in the afternoons." Joey goes over to the window behind the sink and looks out. The sound of the Range Rover starting up thinly muffled by old brickwork and lead lined windows.

"You eat geese?" I say.

"Now and then." Joey says walking back to the table and sipping his beer. "We don't go to the shops too often."

"I don't blame you. I work in a Megamarket; it's like day of the dead in there sometimes. I work nights though, it's not so bad." I take a gulp and look around the kitchen. "Does this belong to Colby?"

"Yeah, everything you see belongs to Colby." Zara says and closes one eye and peers down into her empty bottle. "Another one?" She stands and moves to the fridge. I finish mine with a chug and say yes please. Johnny Wriggles looks at his cigarette and blows smoke rings towards it. Joey just sits and takes it all in. The ceiling overhead creaks with footsteps across the upstairs.

"How many of you live here?"

"Sometimes there's six of us, sometimes there's more. It depends."

"Colby doesn't give out his personal number to many." Johnny says smoke whispering around him. "He must see something in you. Is there something in you?"

"Well, if there is I haven't found it yet." I say and Johnny smiles and says, "Colby can help you with that."

Footsteps on the stairs now and every second I feel like I'm in some kind of surreal play.

And I'm drinking my beer and feeling nervous for a reason I can't figure out. Zara sits down opposite again and smiles at me all soft cheeks and warmth.

Colby Stein walks into the kitchen and seems to absorb everybody's focus.

"Good to see you." He says.

"Thank you." I say not really sure what I'm thanking him for.

"Are you being made welcome?" His voice is quiet but solid.

"Beers and cigarettes," I say, "Ticks all the boxes." And he laughs at this and nods saying "Good, good." He goes over to the fridge and pulls out a bottle of water and takes two thirsty gulps.

"We'll go out for dinner later. Talk about a few things and get to know one another.

CHAPTER TEN

At BURGERME Diner we drink Cokes and order cheeseburgers.

Colby Stein says that waitress over there by the counter will earn minimum wage for forty, fifty, sixty hours a week for the rest of her life or until she's too lame to work at all. There are a million of her and there are a million of you. Same job, same dreams same favourite Spice Girl. Same girlfriend, same boyfriend, same fucking credit rating. And everybody has their lives organised in pretty much the same way that you can mix and match. You earn your money as best as you know how and then you divide it up between all the things that you are told you need and then whatever is left you are allowed to spend on things that you actually want. Your life is being taxed by your mobile phone. You are getting broken down application by application. This is the matrix, the laws, the rules, the regulations.

Our instincts are as dull as clay. We need to drop the ego, drop the super-ego. This fear of consequence is man-made over millennia. It's the first thing man ever made. And it is a fear. When you get down to the grit of it; it is only a fear. A fear of what is going to happen to you. A fear of how you are going to feel. A fear of the fucking consequence. Some people aren't like this though, some people are born resistant to it, and they hold onto their authentic actions and they get called immature and unrealistic. They do not fear the consequences, they struggle but they do not fear. The others though, they will kill you if they have the chance and the sooner the better for them. Do not tip the apple cart. Listen, you are growing up and dying at exactly the same rate, you will never be all of who you can be. There is no whole self to lose. You exist or you live. And you live and you die. There are a million you and you live on.

Colby says we're in the age of information and he was born in 1960 and that it gets harder to keep that fuck-it attitude the older you get. Got married at eighteen got divorced at nineteen got remarried at twenty one and had two kids. One day the house burnt down and killed Kristen Stein and her daughters Sarah and Elizabeth. That's some terrible cards right there he says. This was in Chicago, he says, when I was there. I moved in with my brother and his wife for about a month or so afterwards just so I could find my anchor. And I remember it well, I remember looking for my anchor and realising that it was gone and that it wasn't coming back and this was *the* consequence that would shape me for the rest of my life. That fragile moment in the vapours of your twenties when you're committed to travelling a certain road a certain distance. That's a really draggy moment. Nihilism, hedonism, you choose your flavour all I do is open the store. Open it up wide enough to drive a fucking van through it. I took a van all the way from Chicago to Nevada. I wanted to start again; I wanted to get to San Fran but didn't make it. It just didn't seem that important. When you pass a certain point you start to live and you don't live in the ways you think you will.

Colby says I adopted Joey because of his name. Joey. Like Joey Ramone. Zara was different. I could tell she was a princess from the moment I saw her. She's pure instinct. Do you like The Ramones? Do you know what? They only created Popeye to get kids to eat spinach. Why do you think they invented The Ramones? You've been lied to since before you were born. What my group and I try to do is show another way. Each moment is special and unique and shouldn't be weighed down by what has gone before it.

"That all sounds pretty full on." I say as the waitress deposits plates of burgers and fries in front of us.

"Well, that's the way I see it." Colby says shaking salt over his plate, his bald head catching the light. Outside the damp dusk is becoming a wet evening.

"I'm not asking you to agree with me. Although the very fact that you came to visit us suggests to me that you recognise something of yourself in what you've heard me say."

"It's not that I disagree. It just seems pretty radical."

"It is pretty radical. It's an ideology completely alien to everything that's been instilled in you since you were old enough to process thoughts." He takes a hungry bite of his burger, sauce over spilling out the back of it and onto his plate.

"I mean, I work in a supermarket, I'm not sure I'm a very radical kind of guy."

"Look," he says putting his burger down and looking at me full beam. "You came to my seminar and we spoke after and I gave you a phone number and you called it. There must be a reason that you made those choices."

"I guess so. It just all seems so-"

"What pisses you off?"

"Jesus, how long have you got?"

"I've got all night. What pisses you off?" He runs a couple of fries through a dollop of ketchup round the side of his plate. I take a pull of Coke through the straw.

"Well, everything really; the way society is constantly telling us what to think. The fact that nobody voices an opinion unless it's deemed acceptable in the court of social media. That you can walk into a bar and everybody has the same haircut. That the biggest musicians of a generation come from televised talent shows." I sigh. "I could go on."

"What I'm trying to say to people is that there is another way. And yes, I suppose you could say that is a pretty radical alternative. But we live in a world where you are either swept along with the current or you fight like crazy to go against it and going against anything, any established cultural way of life is by definition radical."

"I get it, I mean, really I do but how can you live like that? Like actually live like that?"

"Well, how are you living now?" Colby pulls the straw out of his glass and takes a swig through the ice. "You drink a lot, maybe smoke a bit of weed, coke, whatever I know what it's like but you are not making any progress. What are you thirty?"

"Twenty nine."

"I was close. What are you going to be doing when you're forty? When you're fifty? When everyone else you know are all happy with their families and their children and their mortgage. You're still going to be unsatisfied. You're still going to be alone."

"So you're saying I should do what? Fuck it all off?"

"I'm saying you should live on your own terms. Do what you want. Take what you want. You only have to pay if they catch you. I did the whole Megamarket thing. There's no glory in it."

He sits there looking at me and I don't even know what to say. I don't know what to think. In a certain twisted kind of way what he is telling me does make a lot of sense. But it seems so far out of left field that I'm not sure that it's even an option. I mean, really.

"Just think about it. That's all." He says and we finish up our meals quietly.

The waitress is back over by the counter talking to the chef and urgently checking somebodies order that has been ballsed up somewhere along the line. Colby pushes his plate away and dumps his scrunched up napkin on top of it.

"Come on." He says standing up. "Let's go." I look at him dumbly for a second.

"You're just going to walk out? Without paying?"

"That's right." And as calmly as anything he begins walking to the front door. I look around mildly panicked and then whispering a fuck it under my breath I follow after him. At the front door I look back but the waitress is still standing there with the chef shaking her head and running her finger up and down some other person's order.

"That wasn't cool." I say catching up to Colby next to the car.

"Yeah, but you did it anyway." He zaps the locks and we get in. "If it had been from that girl that we were stealing it would have been different."

"I wasn't brought up to steal." I say the pissed off rising in my throat half strangling my words so that they come out weak. Colby starts the car and backs out of the parking space and spins it round.

"You were brought up to recite the Lord's Prayer in assembly at school. You were brought being told that Christ died on the cross and was reborn for your sins. If that is the case then you are already covered. If it is a load of horse shit then maybe you should start to question how you were brought up."

We pull out of BURGERME and join the tail of brake lights.

"I don't know man. Still seems pretty fucked up to me."

Colby laughs.

"No blindfold?" I say.

"What?"

"Zara and those guys made me wear a blindfold when they picked me up."

Colby laughs.

"No blindfold." He says.

We drive the rest of the way back in silence. I'm thinking that my parents would be ashamed.

Headlights and brake lights. Forwards and back.

Colby Stein pulls into a motel at the side of the road in the middle of nowhere and kills the engine.

"What are we doing?"

"Just stopping off to see a friend." He says and he leans across me and opens the glove box. He pulls out a small brown envelope wrapped in thick tape. "You coming?" He says as he opens the door and swings out a leg. I know a package of drugs when I see one but I get out anyway.

Colby walks towards the room at the far end and bangs on the door.

"It's open." Says a voice from inside and Colby opens the door.

Inside the television is flickering up on the bracket. Cheap plastic surfaces, wipe clean furniture. A figure sitting on the end of the bed and at first I don't recognise him. Until I see the sunglasses and then I remember him, the blind man from the hotel.

"Lucian, how are you?" Colby asks as he sets the package down on the desk underneath the television.

"Fantastic. Been waiting for you all evening." He says in a plain voice edged with agitation. He doesn't move his head, his face perfectly blank. "Who's that with you?"

"He's with me. He's fine, don't worry about it."

"I'm not worried about it. What have you got me?"

"It's the same as last time."

"Jesus, Colby."

"Yeah, yeah." Colby says and looks over at me and arches his eyebrows framing the slight grin that plays on his lips.

"What's your story?" Lucian asks and it takes me a moment to realise that he's talking to me.

"I…uh… I haven't got much of a story." I say.

"Everybody has a story." Lucian says without moving his head. His face looks dry and creased. "What do you do?"

"I work in Megamarket." I say and I feel squashed by the insignificance of that sentence. "I'm making the rest up as I go along."

"Got yourself another Megamarket boy, eh Colby?"

"Just bouncing around the consequences, Lucian." Colby says and Lucian gives a snort of a laugh.

"Sure you are."

"It makes a change from the same shit different day routine." I say.

"Yeah, well whatever, I don't give a shit."

"If you don't feel like talking, we'll leave you be." Colby says.

"Yeah, good."

Back in the car we pull the door shut behind us and we just sit there in silence.

"My father." Colby says. "Is a difficult man to get to know."

"That's your father?"

"That's my father." And he twists the key in the ignition and aims us back out onto the road.

CHAPTER ELEVEN

The smell hits me as soon as we walk into the kitchen. Zara and Joey standing around the hob a big vat of something is simmering on one of the burners.

"What's going on?" Colby asks.

"Making some tea." Joey answers him without looking up. It doesn't smell like any tea I've ever had before. Zara turns around and smiles.

"How was your dinner?" She asks her voice sounding like a smile.

"It was good." Colby says. "We talked." He goes over to the fridge and pulls a bottle of water. Zara raises an eyebrow at me.

"It was good." I say and Zara smiles.

"Alright, it's ready." Joey says and sips some out of the ladle. "Fucking disgusting."

"What you got going on over there?" I ask moving over and peering into the murky brown of the pan.

"You ever taken magic mushrooms?" Joey asks ladling the liquid into a mix matched collection of cups.

"Sure, at Uni. We just ate them though."

"It's much better this way." He says. Small lumps of chopped up mushrooms float to the surface like fingertips. He picks up a cup and hands it to me. "Colby?" He asks.

"Sure, I'm in."

We go through to the living room, each of us with a steaming cup of foulness in our hands. The place is lit up by candles on every free surface and shadows play up the walls and across the low, beamed ceiling. Ewan is sitting in the rocking chair next to the fire which licks and spits and crackles about the logs that fuel it. He's reading a thin paperback and he looks up as we sit down on the couches and piles of cushions.

"How was dinner?" He asks as Colby sits down in an armchair by the fireplace.

"It was fine." Colby says and takes a sip of his tea and grimaces.

"What are you reading?" I ask him.

"The Metamorphosis." Ewan says.

"I like Kafka." I say.

"I'm sure you do." And he returns his focus to the book.

I take another sip of the tea and look around the room. There's a Ram's head mounted on a board above the fire, its horns curling out to points. Zara is holding her cup in both hands and blowing at the steam.

"Where's Johnny?" Colby asks.

"He's gone out for a walk." Joey says between mouthfuls. I've got an uneasy feeling growing in the base of my chest, I'm not sure that I want to be going on a trip this evening.

"Relax." Zara says as if reading my mind.

"I'm cool." I say and take another gulp, soft chunks of mushroom slop against me teeth and the back of my throat. Colby puts his cup down on the table and settles back in his chair, closing his eyes and sighing softly. I can feel my heart beating in my ribcage. I can feel my pupils growing. My skin feels alive.

Joey sits down, cross legged in front of the fire. The walls of the room are the colour of burnt sugar. I finish the drink and put it down on the table in front of me.

"I'll get you a top up." Zara says springing to her feet and picking up my cup. I don't say anything.

The walls are on fire. Like a room of napalm.

Ben and me sitting on my bed in my room in the halls of residence. Apocalypse Now on the small television in the corner. The Doors are playing The End. The small plastic box empty between us.

The walls are breathing.

I lean my head back and watch the wooden beams, the knots and the grain shimmering and dripping. Out of the corner of my eye, in the doorway a shadow and then Zara puts the cup down in front of me.

"How are you feeling?" Somebody asks. I look around. Colby is looking at me a slight smile on his face. A stab of a paranoid fear. An echo of a thought.

"I'm good." I think I say as the fire twists and reaches and Ewan keeps on reading his book. I watch my hand as it picks up the steaming cup from the table and I drink some more, no longer tasting anything.

Ben is from Bradford or Stafford or somewhere. Says all he used to do was take mushrooms. With his friends in the park.

Joey leans towards the fire and runs his hand through the flame. Zara watches him and laughs. Ewan has become an insect in the rocking chair. His wire framed glasses sprout antennae.

The walls are breathing in time with my own inhale/exhale.

Somewhere, sometime, somebody opens a door.

Hello.

Hello?

Black suit, white shirt, black tie standing in the doorway. No shoes, no socks.

"Hello, Johnny." Colby Stein's voice floats up in the darkness and flickers in the firelight. "Nice and calm Johnny."

"Sure, Colby."

"You want some tea Johnny?" Zara looks up her eyes are black.

"Not for me. Thank you. It's a nice night." He says softly, still standing in the doorway. Joey stands up and goes to the window and tweaks the curtains.

"Full moon." He says.

"Yeah, full moon. Clear sky."

"The moon pulls on the water." Colby says looking directly at me. "Seventy percent of your body is water." Barely a whisper. I can feel my arms start to lift as if on strings. I can hear the fibres of the rocking chair straining.

Napalm explodes a jungle. I close my eyes and watch my own film projected in suggestions of colour.

Open your eyes.

"I'm going up to bed."

"Okay, Johnny."

I feel above myself, above my memories. Like my mind is being stretched up towards the moon. Zara is staring into the fire. Joey turns away from the window and looks up at the ceiling. The Ram's skull is smiling. Ewan reads his book with his antennae twitching from the frame of his glasses. Colby Stein has his eyes closed that trace of a smile still on his lips.

Suddenly the bottom falls out of everything and I take a big gulp of air as the room comes back into focus. Ewan looks up at me, mildly interested and then back to the book. I look around and wonder why Colby Stein owns a farm in the middle of nowhere. I stand up and nobody notices. Everybody in their own private world. I go to the window feeling like I'm floating and pull the curtains open. I can't see the moon. I can't see anything apart from the ghost of my own reflection.

What are you doing?

You are Stacker and everything is joined up. The reflected me stares back with massive dark eyes. I reach out and touch the window and I'm replaced by a reflected hand.

Ben says let's go for a walk.

Through dead streets with diluted music thudding through cheap student brickwork. There's no moon in the park.

The clouds are dripping into one another.

"We are the kings of our own destiny." Colby Stein is at my shoulder. Ewan stands up and folds his book shut, drops it on the table and looks around.

I haven't moved from the couch.

"I'm going to bed." Ewan says and Colby Stein nods. Zara runs her hand up a wooden beam. The fire spits beads of red and orange onto the carpet where they disappear and the edge of my vision goes cloudy. Ewan heads to the stairs.

"I used to stack the shelves." Colby says. "I told you that." And he laughs. "We're the same person."

"I wasn't brought up that way." I hear myself say. "We're not the same person."

"Take it easy." I can feel myself swaying. I can hear Jim Morrison singing.

This is

The

End.

I sit down heavily, watching myself dispassionately like a scientist observing something that he doesn't understand. Somebody says something about the psychedelic experience revealing layers of understanding beneath conscious thought. Zara is talking.

Ben doesn't think there is anything worthwhile after University.

I can't imagine Colby Stein stacking shelves.

I can't imagine Colby Stein using an estate agent.

"How's everyone feeling?" Joey sounds very far away.

"Good."

"Good."

"I don't know."

"Shit. Look at him."

"He's fucked."

"I feel fucked up."

Somebody opens a window and the flames dance up to meet the new oxygen. Somebody blows out a candle and the room goes dark.

The echo of a breath and everything goes dark.

Voice on the end of the phone sounds familiar says hello.

Yeah, hello.

It's your uncle; he's dead.

CHAPTER TWELVE

Airport bars are open twenty four hours a day. People arriving at all hours nobody really knowing what time it is or where they are.

Everybody wanting a drink.

I'm at the bar in Heathrow waiting to catch the overnight to Detroit drinking a Mojito for the hell of it. The plane is delayed because of weather. Nothing vaguer than weather and we'll be lucky to be in the air by midnight. The guy sitting next to me says his name is Arnold, says he produces "Pornographic video movies for distribution on the internet. Those low budget eastern European ones; where the girl gets fucked by the stranger she meets in the street."

"Yeah, I know them." I say as a sudden rainbow of people surge into the bar. The bar staff visibly tense up as up and down their barricade hands and wallets and notes of all the air bound people of the world slap down upon the bar. And in the split of a second everybody is crying out for drinks.

"Do you take the dollar here?" Somebody yells out.

"They actually know each other."

"Who does?"

"The talent, in the movies, they know each other." He's maybe Dutch, maybe German, I'm terrible with accents. "But they're not always in a relationship. Sometimes they are, so that's real sweet. The boys are all in the farm and they get the girls involved."

"The farm?"

"Yes. The Stud Farm, we give them the right medicine to keep them in good enough shape and ready to fire on command."

"You sound like you enjoy your work."

"Yes, of course. Everybody is fucking all the time." He smiles and I notice that he has sleazy eyes. "What do you do?"

"I'm a Stacker."

"What is this?"

"I stack things, you know, in a supermarket, a shelf stacker."

"You like your work?"

"I love it." I say and finish my drink and crunch down some ice. "Who do you think was the last person to smoke a cigarette in here?"

"In here? In this pub?" Arnold looks confused, "How would I know that?" He looks at me with raised eyebrows as people crowd all around us.

"You wouldn't." I say and start laughing.

"You British are crazy."

I'm laughing because at 11:59 PM on June the thirtieth 2007 I was smoking a cigarette in the exact same spot as I'm sitting in tonight. Everybody in the place knew it was coming. We even had a countdown. People who didn't even smoke were lighting up cigarettes at five to midnight just for the kick of it. And then boom, a million cigarettes extinguished as the nation was enveloped in the safe embrace of the smoking ban.

"Do you make much money?" Arnold asks, checking his watch for the thousandth time.

"I get by."

"I make money. The talent makes money. The Penis Enlargement company who sidebar my films make money. It's good work."

"Sure." I say and wait patiently for the crowd to thin out.

"Excuse me sir, do you take the dollar here?" The American cries out again his voice cut with desperation.
Arnold pulls his briefcase up onto his knees and then onto the bar and opens it.

"Look at these." He says and pulls out a sheaf of portrait photos. He hands the pile to me. The top one is of a sad looking girl with a thin face and black hair scraped back cruelly. The next, a blonde with hair in her face and the same sad eyes; the next another blonde who looked like she had been crying.

"These girls don't look very happy." I say flicking through the rest.

"Yes. We take the dollar here." A barman finally engages with the American.

"That's because these were taken before the girls got paid." Arnold laughs and it seems to strike off something inside of me. The American orders two bottles of Budweiser and a straight up Jack and I immediately like him better than Arnold. I put the photographs down on the bar and turn to the American.

"Hey, man, this seat is free. This guy was just leaving." The American looks at me and Arnold looks at me and ever so calmly I pick up the stack of photographs and toss them away onto the floor.

It's never like the movies.

Arnold's face has barely changed from surprise to anger as he punches me in the cheekbone. The tall seat I'm on rocks back under sudden inertia and then rocks me forward again into another jab. I fire back with a straight left which glances pathetically off of his ear as he hits me again in the mouth. This time the seat swings back past the point of no return and I'm on the floor.

And Arnold is down at me.
He gets in two more pistoning punches before two men in high-vis vests and weapons belts are pulling him off me saying, "easy now." I stand up coughing, droplets of blood spraying in front of my eyes like broken pixels. Arnold is being held by two Police Officers and he's struggling, saying, "My pictures. My fucking pictures."

"Calm down sir, just calm down."

"He threw my pictures." He's really mad. One of the Cops bends Arnold's arm up behind him and slams him down onto the bar whilst the other one steps forward and says, "What's this about pictures?"

"He was showing me pictures, sure he was but I didn't throw them anywhere. I dropped them." Meanwhile the American is staring open mouthed at the whole scene before his eyes and a bottle of Budweiser in each of his hands. I look around licking my busted lip; everybody is staring like people do after a bar fight. The barman passes me a towel and I mop up my face.

"Well, what do you want to do?"

"What do you mean?"

"I mean, do you want to press charges?" And then he steps forward again and with his arm on my shoulder he half turns us away and says, "To be honest with you, any act of aggression that takes place inside of an airport is considered terrorism."

"Oh yeah?"

"Yeah, this guy has just got himself in a lot of bother. If you want to press the additional charge of assault, then you're going to have to come and make a statement."

"I just want to have a drink and catch my flight."

"Where you headed?"

"Detroit. Well I'm flying to Detroit and then crossing to Canada. Uncle's funeral."

"Sorry to hear that."

"Thanks. If you can just get this guy out of here, that'll do just fine."

"What's this about pictures?"

"They're down there." I say and point out the splayed out sheets of photographs of sad girls. The cop shakes his head and stoops to pick them up. The other one is shuffling Arnold out, everyone's getting bored now. I pick up the seat and sit back down and turn to look at the American. "Can I grab one of those?" He looks at me and sits down on the newly vacant chair next to me. He puts one of the bottles in front of me and knocks back his Jack.

"Thanks." I say and take a drink.

"That was nuts." He says, "What was all that?"

"Nothing much."

"I've never been in a fight."

"Yeah, well they hurt." And then I add, "That guy was a prick. It's about accepting consequence and dealing with it." Words without thinking, words that seems to spark something behind the guy's eyes and he says. "You're a consequence man."
I put my beer down carefully on the bar and turn to look at him. "You know Colby Stein?"

"I don't know him, I mean I've met him, I've been following his seminar tour. He's an inspiration." He goes on his voice rising in excitement. "He's changed the way I live my life. Inspirational. Do you know Colby?"

"I don't know if I'd say I know him. I've spent some time with him and his group." My blood on the neck of the bottle. "He's got some pretty out there ideas, that's for sure." Darkening as it congeals.

The American introduces himself as Bill from Ohio and says he's followed Colby Stein all over the States and he came to Britain after walking out on his wife and kid "because they didn't get it." Says he saw Colby first in London and then in Birmingham. He calls it Birming-*ham*. He says he's going back home to raise up some more cash and Colby has said he can join the group. "Life is a series of moments each one precious and unique and each one shouldn't be weighted by the previous."

I buy the next round of Budweisers.

People keep dripping into the bar.

At around ten thirty I go out to the gents. My face puffed up purple around the eye in the mirror. A split in my lip filled with sticky black blood. Blood on my teeth. I wash up as best I can and dab at myself until the basin is filled with compacted and newly pink paper towels. I turn thirty soon and I'm getting beaten up in airport bars. I am a walking overdraft. I am Stacker.

I walk out of the toilets just in time to hear them calling my flight to the gate. The weather has improved. Turns out that Bill from Ohio is catching the same plane and we walk there together him with his smart carry-on luggage me with my hands in my pockets. I tell him that the last time I flew was about seven years ago for my cousins christening. Bill tells me that his daughter got christened last year. He tells me things were different back then.

We line up at the gate with our boarding passes in our hands. The family in front look at me with a bleary cocktail of fear and disgust and tuck their children tightly in front of them. The staff at the gate smile as I hand over my pass and my ticket and my passport. Their demeanour never changes, their smiles never slip.

When we reach the plane door Bill shakes my hand and says "Have a nice flight." As he is ushered to the left and me to the right.

CHAPTER THIRTEEN

We could disappear at thirty three thousand feet somewhere over the ocean and become celebrities. People would know us from our passport pictures and old school photos. For a week or until something else more interesting or fucked up happened we would be the centre of the world. Conspicuous by our absence. That's what happened to that plane awhile back. Bad things have to happen for people to throw up a prayer for you.

The woman next to me has the complexion of a handbag and has been asleep since take off.

My mum said; "I can't go because you know why." After all the jazz about my father uncle John, his brother, wanted nothing more to do with my mum. Fair enough, I suppose. Now Uncle John is dead and my brother is in Australia and it falls to me to represent. I emailed Aunt Marie my flight details and she arranged to come and pick me up. I hope she knows we're running late. Britain is five hours ahead of Detroit, I left in the middle of the night and I will arrive in the middle of the night.

At thirty three thousand feet you don't order the American style fun sized cans of beer you order the little bottles of white wine and two at a time and you drink them hard and fast whether you like them or not. All around me people are turning off their personal lights and pulling sleep masks over their eyes. The handbag next to me is snoring through her unclasped mouth. Three hours in, somewhere above the Atlantic and my face hurts. I'm half cut and restless. I finish off the second bottle and tuck it in the pocket of the chair in front of me, which is rudely tipped as far back as it can go. I buzz for the stewardess.

"Is everything alright?" She says when she arrives all teeth and perfume.

"I'd like some more wine please." I grin at her trying to match the wideness of her plastic smile but I can feel my lip beginning to tear itself apart so I stop. I can see doubt in her eyes. "I got attacked at the airport." I say, "A terrorist incident. Apparently."

"Oh, I'm sorry to hear that." The flinch after the word terrorist is momentary. She could probably break my arm if I went at her with one of the plastic forks. "I'll be right back."

"Thank you." And she swishes away down the aisle to the back of the plane where they stow the refrigerated drinks trolley. In less than a minute she comes back with three little bottles nested in her elegant fingers.

"Enjoy." She says her perfect teeth flashing through the gloom.

I watch the picture of our plane unspooling its red line on the screen that's set into the back of the seat in front. We're halfway over the ocean now, Britain and Ireland as far behind as America is in front. This is as far away from civilization as you can get. I suppose that back in the day flying was seen as glamorous, something for the wealthy and privileged to keep to themselves. Now it's just an excuse to get high altitude drunk. Apparently this high up, the effects of alcohol double or even triple in some cases, I just have a headache though. Some people do this every week. Back and forth, gaining hours dropping hours, constantly time travelling. Fat futures and thin blood.

And they don't let you on until they've taken your lighter. At every airport around the world somebody has access to vast stockpiles of cigarette lighters and books of matches with Airport hotel logos on them. I'm starting to get that scratchy nicotine craving. Synapses in my brain are snapping at each other telling my nervous system that everything will be okay if we can just fire up a Lucky Strike. It's a bust up here though.

Donny Brinklow said; "Hello, Donny Brinklow speaking, how can I help?" In his best telephone voice.

"Mr Brinklow, it's me." I said.

"I thought we had left it that I would contact you." He said.

"Yes we did but something has come up and I thought you should know in case you tried to contact me and couldn't."

"Go on…"

"My Uncle has died and he lives in Canada so I will be out of the country for a bit."
There was a pause and then he said. "Okay. Sorry to hear that. When will you be back?"

"The middle of next week I think. I can let you know."

"If you can let me know that would be fine. Is there anything else?"

"No."

Uncle John had met Marie when she was travelling around Europe and it was one of those loves at first sight type deals that don't happen anymore. They had lived in London for a bit before Marie decided that she wanted a child and she wanted to have it back home to be near her family. Uncle John was a teacher and had said fine, he had always wanted to teach abroad.

And now at fifty five he was dead from a massive heart attack leaving behind my Aunt Marie and cousin Bonny who was about ten years younger than me and studying to herself become a teacher.

I don't even know what time it is but I've got that high altitude sadness humming through my head. My face hurts and I just want to sleep.

CHAPTER FOURTEEN

I stride through Detroit International with my bag slung over my shoulder and a cigarette clamped between my teeth. I'm in that precious gap between being blurry drunk and brutally hung over. I need a drink of water and a cigarette.

It's the middle of the night all over again and Marie and Bonny are waiting sleepy eyed at the arrivals gate. They smile thin sad smiles when they see me and both of them wave.

"How was your flight?" Marie says embracing me at the elbows and kissing me on the cheek. "We heard about all the delays." And then, "What happened to your face?"

"It wasn't the best but it was alright. There was a bit of a misunderstanding back in England, it's not as bad as it looks. It'll come off in the shower" I say hugging her back. "How are you doing?" I step back and look at her; she is pale and her eyes watery, she looks thin, like she has spent every mealtime crying instead of eating.

"We're doing okay." She says and she must have realised how unconvincing she sounds because she attempts a full beam smile which stutters and falls short around the eyes.

"How are you Bonny?" I say and hug my cousin.

"I'm okay." She says. In times of bereavement people always say that they are okay even when they definitely are not.

Outside of the terminal I smoke a cigarette, bumming a light off a man with a limp. Marie has gone to get the car and Bonny stays standing next to me.

"We're glad you came." She says, "How are things with you?"

"Things are the same as always, nothing much changes over there."

"How is Rob? Do you speak to him much?"

"He's alright I think, it's hard to tell. He's still in Australia, he manages a bar out there."

"That sounds nice." Bonny is craning her neck looking out for Marie. I crush out my cigarette under my foot and look around myself. Even in the middle of the night and I still don't know what time it actually is, the airport is busy. Giant American cars cruising up the one way system pulling in and out of the drop off/pick up point. Taxi drivers hauling fat suitcases into the backs of their cabs. Nicotine deprived smokers firing up duty free cigarettes with shaking hands.

Everybody going somewhere.

"Here she is." Bonny says and waves at a dark blue Pontiac with Marie behind the wheel. Marie angles the car into a space by the curb and I pick up my bag again and climb into the back with it as Bonny gets in the front.

"Have you got your passport to hand?" Marie asks looking in the rear view mirror, "For the border."

"Yeah, I got it right here." I say and tap my jacket pocket.

It's a quirk of geography that Detroit is further north than the part of Canada which it borders. We drive out of the airport complex and merge with the traffic heading downtown. Rundown trailer parks on each side of the freeway muddled with burnt out patches of industry. Detroit fell hard when the financial world imploded and is still awaiting redemption. Bonny reaches back and hands me a bottle of water.

We pull off of the freeway before we hit the downtown loop and head towards Mexico Town. Here desolation and menace run free amongst boarded up houses and crudely graffitied tenement blocks. You can smell the edge of America, that rotten fruit smell that comes with the end of empire. Cars are propped up on bricks, their wheels long since pawned or stolen. A couple of stray dogs chase each other across the street in front of us causing Marie to step hard on the brakes.

"This town has a dog problem." She says shaking her head and tapping the wheel nervously. Signs overhead point us towards the border crossing and after a series of staggered left and right turns we pull up into the line-up for non-commercial vehicles. At this time of night there aren't too many people ahead of us and we don't have to wait long.

When we get to the booth at the end of the line Marie and Bonny present their passports and Marie says; "Two Canadians and one British."
The man in a dark blue uniform takes a cursory look at the two Canadian passports and then says, "Let me see his." I lean forward and hand him my passport through the open window. He withdraws back into his booth and studies it under the light. Finally satisfied he passes it back to Marie who hands it to Bonny who hands it to me.

"Have a nice night." Says the Border Control Officer and he raises the barrier in front of us and we drive onto the Ambassador Bridge and onward to Canada.

Windsor, Ontario lies across the river from Detroit and was my Uncle's home for over twenty years. Marie drives us up and down streets and boulevards with French sounding names until we pull off of the main roads and into the suburbs. The roads here are more open than in the built up areas with parks and baseball diamonds and playing fields running into small plazas of Sports Bars and Nail Salons.

Eventually we pull up the driveway and we're home. Marie presses a button on her key fob and the automatic garage door hums as it opens. She slowly pulls inside and parks up next to Uncle John's SUV.

"There's beers in the fridge, help yourself." Marie says as she puts her keys down on the counter in the kitchen. Bonny goes over to the fridge and pulls out two bottles of lager.

"I don't mean to be rude but I really need to go to bed. I haven't been sleeping very well recently."

"Of course, Aunt Marie." I say and I give her another hug, "Thank you for getting me. Sorry it's so late."

"That's not your fault sweetheart and it's my pleasure. I'm glad you could come." She says and pours herself a glass of water from a jug in the fridge. "Bonny will show you your room when you're ready. I'll see you in the morning."

"Night mum." Bonny says kissing her on the cheek.

"Night princess."

Bonny and I sit at the kitchen table and drink beers. She tells me all about her teaching course and how she is so optimistic for her future. But even as she tells me all of her plans I can tell that her every other thought keeps returning to her Dad and his sudden cruelly conceived loss.

"I just can't believe he's gone." She says eventually, studying her bottle of Labatt Blue. "I don't think that it's sunk in yet."

"It takes time." I say. My father has been in a coma for nearly twenty years and it's only been in the last five years or so that I've reached any kind of level of acceptance. Of course my Mum has yet to reach anything approaching closure. "One day at a time."

"Do you still work at that supermarket?" She says wiping her eyes and fetching two more bottles. Over here bottles of beer are screw top.

"Megamarket, yeah, I don't recommend it."

"Oh, Megamarket. They've just opened one of those downtown." Megamarket will not be satisfied until it owns the world. "I'm thinking about getting a temporary job there over Christmas. They're already advertising jobs. Do you like it?"

"Like I say; I don't recommend it." We both laugh.

One day at a time.

CHAPTER FIFTEEN

We're all standing in the cemetery in sad little clusters and rows as the wind blows cancer in at us from across the river. Everybody is talking in quiet little bursts that taper off before anything much is really said.

I didn't bring my suit with me because it stills stinks of sick from Mike's wedding. Yesterday, when I told Aunt Marie that I needed to go into town to buy a new one she told me I was about John's size and I should just pick one off of his rail. So here I am with a marked up face wearing a dead man's suit and feeling pretty punk and low about the whole thing. Marie and Bonny both agreed that I look very smart.

We're in that awkward nowhere time waiting for the hearse to arrive. I'm stood next to Bonny and silently debating whether it would be acceptable to smoke a cigarette. Marie is talking to her sister Barbara and nervously tapping her foot on the edge of the tarmac. Behind us the grave is freshly dug and as deep as it is final. The cemetery is on the top of a mild hill and offers a fine view of the Detroit skyline with all its semi empty skyscrapers and office blocks. Smack bang in the middle of it the phallus of the General Motors Building rises above the surrounding grime. It is a grey day on both sides of the border and nobody wants to be anywhere.

In the distance the black hearse pulls into the cemetery and makes its way slowly up the lane towards us. There is that collective breath that comes when you get the first sighting of the coffin and you can see jaws tightening and eyes tearing up and glazing over. Bonny dabs at her face with a tissue and I decide against the cigarette. Marie comes back and puts her arm around her daughter who reciprocates. I never know what to do with my hands in these situations so I mate them behind my back and rock slightly on my heels.

The Priest wanders over in his white smock and says some quiet words to Marie who says thank you as her eyes brim over with tears and the professional Pall Bearers ready themselves at the back of the hearse. People begin to make their way to the grave and there are more tears. Marie takes Bonny by the arm and I follow on behind them as a sharp gust blows at our faces. Apart from my aunt and my cousin the only other person I know is my Grandma who is bat shit senile and keeps calling me Rob. After the fourth or fifth time I stopped correcting her. I am Stacker and I will take my brother's name if it is easier.

They bring the coffin over, carried on top of broad, well-practised shoulders and place it on a low slung frame by the side of the grave and step away from it bowing their heads and clasping their hands at their groins.

"I just want to look at it forever." Aunt Marie says in shuddering sobs. "I don't want him to go." But she knows as well as anybody that the man she loved has already long since gone. I know what she means though, that clinging onto some last residual tangible moment. We all stand there grimly as Marie and Bonny cry into each other's shoulders. The professionals thread straps under the box and all around the group people are convulsing into tears.

I'm thinking about the time my dad and Uncle John took me and Robert crabbing off the end of Cromer pier. I was maybe seven and Rob was nine and we were both excited about seeing Uncle John. I remember him arriving at our caravan wearing a Polo shirt with the sun behind making him look all angelic and made of light. We piggy-back raced up the pier, me on my dad's back and Rob on Uncle John's. We got to the bar at the end of it and I remember thinking that although most people don't, we would probably be able to live forever if we could just hold onto this particular moment. Mum and Aunt Marie were back in the caravan talking about cross stitch and quilting or some other unimportant thing and I remember thinking that they were missing out on some kind of eternal magic out there on the end of the pier. These moments magnify until they're bigger than anything else when somebody dies, those special once in a lifetime moments.

And then they get sucked back into the nothing that surrounds them.

Gone.

They each grab an end of one of the straps whilst the Priest murmurs on about souls starting out on a new journey and how each moment that we remember John is a moment that he has given us and that how he truly believes that we are all destined to return to God's rightful flock. And I'm thinking that if he carries on I'm going to have to say something. But of course I never will. And they begin to lower him down into the grave and fresh tears are sprung with everybody leaning on each other for support and comfort. Somebody comes round, as the Priest carries on with the last rites and hands us all a single red rose and we huddle around the grave and in turn we toss the flowers one by one down on top of the coffin.

I want to be cremated.

The Wake is held in the function room of a local Hotel. At the far end of the room people are already lining up at the buffet table and stacking their plates with triangular sandwiches and skewers of chicken and lengths of cut vegetables.

"So, what is it that you do?" I'm talking to Marie's brother Alan.

"I work in a supermarket." It always feels embarrassing to say and has grown in humiliation the older I get.

"Oh, really? Which one?"

"A Megamarket, back in England." I can see in his eyes that he has automatically lowered his opinion of me. I don't blame him.

"Ah, Megamarket; one of those has just opened over here." He says and then adds, "Do you enjoy it?" Standard question. Even if you don't yourself, people always define you by the job you do.

"It's alright, I mean, I just never figured out what to do. I have a degree it's just a question of working out what to do with it." Always that need to justify myself.

"I see." I can see in his eyes that he's thinking; waster. He's probably right. I excuse myself and go back up to the bar before he can ask any more questions.

I order a Bloody Mary which the barman makes with half arsed effort and then I stand there and just look. People are just milling about as is the fashion at these events; subdued and low key. A guy of about my age comes over with a mountainous plate of food and orders a bottle of Blue.

"How are you doing?" He asks, his hair is choppy and sticking up at all angles, his suit jacket is creased and he isn't wearing a tie.

"I'm doing alright. How about you?"

"You're British eh?"

"That's right."

"Nice; good for you." He puts his bottle of beer down on the bar and wipes his hand across his jacket and sticks it out to me. "I'm Scott." I shake his hand and introduce myself. "How did you know the deceased?" He asks.

"John was my dad's brother, my Uncle." I say and finish my drink. "What about you?"

"I'm a friend of the family. Very sad, so sudden." He lets his eyes drift down to the carpet reflecting on the sadness and the suddenness. Across the room Bonny is doing the small chat funeral thing, the light from the window flows in from the window behind her and I'm reminded of my Uncle John for a moment. I knock back the rest of my drink.

"I'm going for a smoke." I say to nobody in particular but by default to Scott.

"I'll come with." Scott says and plucks two sandwiches from his plate.

In the designated smoking area I slouch against the brickwork and light up.

"What happened to your face?" Scott asks me.

"Just a bit of bother at the airport." I say, "No big deal." Scott hasn't sparked up yet.

"Hey," He says, "Do you want to go and smoke a joint?" And he tips a wink.

"Now?" I say immediately warming to the idea.

"Sure." Says Scott. "I got some pre-rolls." He grins and I'm thinking why the fuck not? "Come on." He says and starts walking around the side of the hotel. I follow him thinking that I'm pretty sure that this is a good idea. We duck into the alcove of an emergency exit and Scott pulls a short, fat joint out of a crumpled deck of smokes and fires it up.

"British Columbia." He says, "The best weed." And he jets smoke out of his nostrils and passes it over and leans back against the wall.

"What do you do?" He asks.

"I work at Megamarket."

"Cool, man. One of those just opened in town."

"Yeah, so I hear." I say through a rough cough.

"I'm thinking about applying."

"So is my cousin, do you know her?"

"Who?"

"My cousin, Bonny." I say passing the joint back to him.

"Uh, not really." He says and looks away.

"How did you say you knew my uncle?" I ask him, something not quite tallying up. Scott lets out a deep sigh.

"Okay, so here's the thing." He says taking two quick pulls. "I didn't know your uncle." He looks at me out of the corner of his eye and passes me the joint.

"So why are you here?"

"It's just a thing I do, man. I don't mean nothing by it."

"What do you mean it's a thing you do? You get high at funerals of people you don't know?"

"I don't always get high." He says and the sun peers out from behind a cloud. "It's called funeral crashing." He says sighing again.

"You crash funerals?"

"Yeah."

"Why?" I'm starting to feel very stoned. I don't know if I'm supposed to be pissed off about this. It just seems funny.

"For the food, man. Free food, free booze. Nobody ever knows everybody at these things. It's a good gig."

"That's fucked up." I pass him back the joint and start laughing. Scott starts laughing too. The sun goes back into hiding.

"Are you pissed off?" He asks when our laughter tapers off.

"I don't know, man. How often do you do it?"

"Most days." He says and we both start laughing again. "Are you going to tell?"

"So this is like your job?"

"I don't know. I guess." He crushes out the joint under his heel. "I'm trying to go straight though." He says earnestly. "That's why I'm applying to Megamarket." He says and he rubs his eyes. They look shot through with blood. "Are you going to tell?"

"Tell who?"

"I don't know; your family?"

"No, man. I'm not going to tell anybody. I think they have enough to deal with at the moment." A wave of confused sadness butts up to me and I suddenly feel ashamed about getting stoned at my uncle's funeral.

"Do you want me to leave?"

"Not really. I don't care. I've got to go back inside though."

"I'll come with." He says blinking his red eyes and we both walk back round to the front of the hotel. An elderly couple dressed in funeral black are shuffling out of the automatic doors. I don't have any idea who they are and I wonder if they're crashers as well. Shit, as far as I know three quarters of these people could be crashers. Scott taps me on the shoulder before we go inside and says; "I'm sorry, man."

"It's cool." I say. "I think you should keep doing this though."

"You think I *should* keep doing this?" He asks his voice murky with weed and confusion.

"Don't go to Megamarket." I say. "They'll eat your soul in there."

"Oh." Scott says.

We walk back into the function room and I thumb my top button open and loosen my tie. Bonny and Marie are sitting at a round table in the corner surrounded by friends and family. Me and Scott go and sit at the bar and order bottles of beer.

At some point Bonny comes and sits with us and looks at me quizzically and I kiss her on the cheek. She seems okay.

Everybody either leaves or gets wasted.

CHAPTER SIXTEEN

I wake up from a dream about facing up and for a couple of seconds I don't know where I am. The digital clock next to me says 05:56 and it all comes back to me. I sit up in bed and wait and see what I'm dealing with. All things told I'm feeling alright. I swing my legs off the bed bunching up the blankets in the process and yawn and stretch. I pull on my jeans and finish off the glass of water next to the bed and flip on the light. The spare room is quietly decorated and apart from the family photos on top of the dressing table I could be in any spare room anywhere in the world.

The spare room is downstairs in the basement something which holds significant novelty value for a Brit whose only experience of basements comes from the damp rubbish packed one in the house where I spent my second year of University.

I pad my way upstairs and into the kitchen. Aunt Marie's jacket is slung over the back of one of the chairs and her clutch bag is toppled over on the table along with her earrings and necklace. The house is quiet, in fact the whole world is quiet and it feels as if I'm the only one in it.

I make myself a coffee and quietly go back downstairs and into the computer room. Just for the hell of it I log onto my Facebook account and see what's going on in the world of virtual friends and things that don't count.

I try to avoid Facebook for the same reasons I try and avoid television; it just doesn't seem real. People have the mentality that just because they can share their thoughts on the weather and inform people of what they had for dinner, that the rest of the world is obliged to pay attention. People are getting dumber I think to myself as I scroll through my newsfeed. This is why there will never been any kind of meaningful revolution in the western hemisphere, people are too easily distracted and too easily caught up in the latest trend or fucking hashtag. I think Colby Stein, for all of his bluster and hyperbole, might have a point. Maybe the answer is to fuck it. To fuck all of it. Individuality is not a desirable character trait in this day and age. People take their cues from reality television and the ultimate aim is to be good looking and stupid. Anything of substance is to be avoided at all costs.

I have one new message. I click on the speech bubble at the top right hand corner of the screen. It's from Zara;

> Hey, how r u? Hope the funeral went OK. I'm back in the states, long and boring story... Do u want to meet up? I'm going to be at Niagara Falls on Wednesday if u r anywhere near there? Let me know... Love Zara xx

I sip at my coffee and think that I would quite like to visit Niagara Falls and that I would quite like to see Zara and why not get the train there tomorrow morning. Sure it would mean missing my flight home but in the grand scheme of things that is hardly a deal breaker. I could always get a different flight home and isn't Toronto fairly near the Falls?

I type back;

> Hey Zara, sure that sounds fun… Will get the train tomorrow morning? Meet you by the water at around about mid-day? X

And hit send. Fuck the consequence.

For a minute or so I carry on scrolling through all the status updates that my friends have posted until my eyes ache through the sheer monotony of it all and I log off and for a moment I just sit there. I go to the news website and scan through the headlines.

A man dies after being tasered by the Police who caught him in an act of cannibalism.

The Skinheads take another seat off of the government in some nowhere town by-election.

An East Anglian farmer is found in a shallow grave, death by shotgun blast.

Russia continues to amass troops east of the Ukraine border.

I turn the whole thing off and for a while I just sit there sipping at my coffee and staring at the blank screen, comfort in the void of nothingness.

When I've finished my coffee I take it upstairs and quietly set it down in the sink and then I go out into the yard to smoke.

The sun is starting to break through the clouds which had thickened overnight. The pool has acquired more leaves and the birdfeeder stands at its side like a sad naked tree. With the cigarette between my teeth I go over to the shed and open it. I don't know if I'm surprised or not to find that it is set out almost exactly to the item like my father's shed. I smile sadly at this. I balance the cigarette on the concrete step up to the shed door and go inside. The bird food is at the back of the workbench just as it is in the old man's shed. I shake my head and laugh quietly at the two brothers, now gone and half gone.

Aunt Marie doesn't bother getting up for breakfast. Bonny takes her a glass of water and some Aspirin while I scramble some eggs.

I tell Bonny, as we eat, that I'm going to take a walk around town today and take an early train to Niagara Falls in the morning. Bonny says that sounds fun and that she would come with me if things were different but that she just wants to stay with her mum. After another cigarette and a shower I put my jacket on and leave the house heading in no direction in particular.

It's not that I don't want to stay and support my cousin and my Aunt; it's just that I am unable. When I've been around people for too long I kind of shut down and withdraw and become pretty morose. I don't know why.

I never used to be like this.

I'd walked for maybe a mile and then I saw it; massive and brick built with a huge expanse of parking lot and a steady stream of incoming traffic. Megamarket, its distinctive and friendly logo designed to reassure and engage customers of all ages with its familiarity.

Walking up to its entrance I'm amazed by the sheer size of the place, dwarfing anything we have back home, it's as if Megamarket as an entity has swallowed several of its smaller competitors. It sits there unashamed by its vastness and cathedral like towers and spires. The sign above the constantly opening and closing automated doors reads; "Megamarket welcomes you to Megamarket, Windsor" In its trademark shade of green. Before I realise what's happening I'm inside, walking on autopilot.

It's like they drug the air.

I remember that I once read some conspiracy theory about how they had put fluoride in all the water mains in North America because fluoride makes you more malleable and susceptible to marketing ploys or dodgy policy. Supposedly in the fifties the government had gotten all the big bosses of commerce to quietly buy into it and then the world of advertising went supernova. Before anybody knew what was happening everybody was blindly consuming whatever they were told. The problem is that they fill the world with so many different shades of horse shit that it becomes impossible to know what is real and what is hoax or flight of fancy. A climate of fear controlled by an atmosphere of paranoia and somebody somewhere is regulating it all.

I've picked up a shopping basket and find myself ambling up and down the aisles, looking at nothing in particular. A giant swimming pool sized container filled with cuddly Father Christmas' appears in front of me with a sign screaming out "Half Priced Santa Claus!" It's October. Maybe this is why I have grown to loathe Christmas. Every shop and retail outlet shoving it down our throats the moment that summer dies.

I carry on walking around in some kind of daze. All around me people seem to be in the same state; just blindly picking up things and putting them in their trolleys, over here they call them karts.

This Megamarket sells more than just groceries. It sells everything.

Ride on Lawnmowers.

Hunting rifles.

Sex toys.

Looking down at my basket I'm alarmed to find that I have filled it with whole load of crap that I have no intention of buying. I drop the basket disgusted. In front of me there is a huge stack of wide spined books. The sign in front of them says; "100 year diary." In front of the stack a girl dressed in the familiar striped shirt and apron of the Megamarket bottom rung is standing with an open copy of the diary on a display table. She sees me staring vacantly at the book on her table.

"Can I interest you in a one hundred year diary, exclusive to Megamarket?" She asks smiling the bright strap on smile of a product demonstrator.

"I don't think I'm going to live that long and I haven't got that much to say really."

"I'm sure that's not true." She says, her smile widening, even her eyes look happy.

"No. It's definitely true."

"The idea is that you pass it down to your children and them in turn to their children. Imagine the joy on your great, great grandchild's face when he or she receives a diary that you yourself have started." She says without missing a beat and rifles through the book for effect.

"I don't think I'm going to have any children." I say and then add; "I mean the world is overcrowded enough as it is." Again that feeling as if I have to justify myself.

For a split second I imagine smashing her in her pretty made up face with one of her hundred year diaries and then I blink the thought to the back of my mind and back away slowly with sweat beading at my temples.

I spin around suddenly gripped by a terrible fear and realise that I'm completely lost. Over the public address system a disembodied voice fills the air.

"Twelve cans of Haricot beans for the price of six down grocery one, get them while you can. Your Megamarket, your world."

I see myself crouched down in full uniform stacking cans of economy canned ham.

I panic.

I orientate myself back to the giant vat of Father Christmas' and without knowing why I grab one by his soft black boot and head back towards the front of the store at a sprint. Nobody even looks up.

Outside I collapse onto a bench and hyperventilate until I feel able to smoke a cigarette. I set the soft toy down on the bench next to me it's dead eyes looking at me as if to say "What the fuck was all that about?"

I don't even know.

As Bonny opens the front door I thrust the Father Christmas at her and say; "Happy Christmas." In my biggest and fakest voice.

"What the fuck?" She says, "It's October."

"I know, Christmas comes earlier each year." I say and give her a hug. "How are you doing? How's your mum?"

"I'm doing okay. Mum's still in bed. Where did you go?" And we go through into the kitchen where a cup of coffee and a Harry Potter book sit next to each other on the table. I went to Megamarket. Just to have a look. It's pretty massive."

"I know, eh?"

Aunt Marie doesn't get out of bed for the rest of the day.

CHAPTER SEVENTEEN

As soon as I get off the train at Niagara Falls I'm hit by the cold. The sort of cold that scythes through your jacket and your skin and your muscles and settles deep in your bones. A massive panoramic shot of the Falls in all their splendour welcomes me to town as I find my place within the disembarking stream of passengers and head towards the exit. Inside the main station building I stow my bag in one of the lockers and head out onto the street with my pale hands shoved deep in my pockets and my collar rolled up. If this is a Canadian October I would hate to stick around for a January.

Outside the station is one of those big maps with a red arrow saying *you are here*. After a quick scan of it I am orientated with enough confidence to head out towards the Falls themselves which look to be maybe a mile away. At this point the town itself doesn't look anything special, the usual run of smoking shops and overpriced souvenir vendors broken up occasionally by various bars and restaurants. I keep walking grimly into the headwind that brings tears to my eyes and pinches my face. I don't really know how I'm going to find Zara but I keep on walking with the blind faith that things will probably work out in the end.

After a while I start to pick up signs directing me to the Falls and I start to feel a bit more confident about the vague plan that was set in motion when I said goodbye to Marie and Bonny outside Windsor rail terminal at half past seven this morning. I still don't take out a cigarette to smoke reluctant to let the harsh wind burn my fingers. I walk with my head down quickly and slaloming between the surges of pedestrians that walk against me.

The closer I get the more surreal the town becomes. It's like walking into some kind of Hollywood/theme park hybrid. Plastic facades mask the majority of buildings, one of them done up like the Empire State Building with a plastic King Kong gripping it's bird shit specked spire. What that has to do with the world's most famous waterfall I know not. Everywhere I look there is some kind of dollar attraction or museum trying to grab at my wandering attention. I didn't expect this, any of it. Obviously Niagara Falls is one of the most visited tourist destinations in the world and I should have expected it but I just thought that something of such monolithic beauty would have somehow retained some kind of class. Everything has that tired plastic end of season faded glory feel to it.

I press on.

At the end of the strip they come into view. Massive and powerful and staggering. I trot across the main street that T-bones at the end of the strip that I was just on and for a few moments I just stare. Millions of gallons gushing at full pelt down and down and downward onto the hard angles of ever corroding rocks and boulders and splashing back up into fine mist that whips and flies. And I'm staggered. Shaped in a stretched out horseshoe and stopping for nothing. This is one of those rare moments when I wish I carried a camera. For several minutes I just stand there in dumb admiration lost of all thoughts of stacking shelves and of death and isolation. As if all of it can just cartwheel and tumble and crash down to the bottom and smash into dust upon the rocks and be forever lost in the mist.

"Hey, you, over here." I turn around and see Zara standing under the canopy of some place called Café Tropical and I wave letting the wind bite at my fingers. She is smiling and I think again how pretty she looks. I cross the road and canter over to her.

"How are you doing?" She asks as she hugs me and kisses me on the cheek.

"I'm alright, I'm cold but I'm alright. How are you?" I say looking over her shoulder into Café Tropical. The place is done up like a rain forest; big plastic tree trunks stand sentry at the doorway and the glass frontage is silhouetted along the bottom half by tigers and toucans and long waves of grass. None of it has anything to do with Niagara Falls.

"Come on inside." She says, "Lucian's here." She leads me through the front door and we politely brush off the advances of the establishment greeter. Zara leads me through to the back portion of the place weaving between tables and booths lined with bamboo. Smack bang in the middle is a giant aquarium where dozens of brightly coloured tropical fish swim around like a migraine. Lucian is sitting bolt upright in his beige suit with his sunglasses on. Zara sits down next to him and me opposite them. His only acknowledgement of me is a slight tilt of his chin.

"How's it going Lucian?" I ask looking directly into his ageless face. He makes no answer and Zara gives a little embarrassed smile. There are two cups of thick black coffee steaming in the middle of the table, Lucian's is untouched. A sharp eyed waitress clocks me as a new arrival and hurries over brandishing a menu and a welcome smile.

"Welcome to Café Tropical." She says putting the menu down in front of me, I notice that there are two more in front of Zara and Lucian which are closed and look completely untouched. "Can I get you something to drink?"

"Just coffee for now, thank you."

"I'll be right back with that." And she scampers off.

"How was the funeral? What happened to your face?" Zara asks picking up her coffee cup with both hands and blowing on it. Lucian remains still as a statue.

"As good as these things can be I guess. I ignored the potential of consequences. It went well." The walls are painted in rainforest scenes and ambient noises of the jungle cheep and chirp sporadically.

"How come you guys are over here? I thought the plan was to stay in Britain?" The waitress comes back with one cup of coffee balanced on a tray and sets it down in front of me. I thank her and begin ripping the tops of the sachets of sugar and dumping them in. Zara waits until the waitress is out of earshot before saying; "Lucian didn't like the gear over there."

"The gear?"

"The smack, the heroin." She says quietly behind a cupped hand.

"Oh." I stir the three sugars into my coffee the spoon chiming off the rim of the cup.

"We're connected up in Toronto. There's a guy coming down, going to take him back to Buffalo."

"What about you?" I ask blowing at my coffee.

"I thought I'd hang with you for a bit, see if we can't get us some kicks Canadian style."

"What's your story Lucian?" I ask across the table. He clears his throat and very slowly and deliberately he reaches up and takes off his sunglasses. I flinch slightly and some of my coffee spills over burning my finger tips and staining the table. Where you and I have eyeballs Lucian has puckered empty sockets and without his dark glasses his face is not much more than the shape of a skull wrapped tight in yellow waxy skin. He clears his throat again and says. "I used to gamble a lot."

"Oh, yeah?" I say trying not to sound totally freaked out.

"Yeah. Now I take a lot of drugs. And soon, God willing, I'll be shot of this whole stinking rock. Until then I intend to obliterate as much of myself as I can."

Zara rolls her eyes at me as if this is all playing happy families.

"Zara, my dear, what is the time?" He asks his voice coarse and breaking.

"It's just coming up to one."

"Fucker should be here soon." He says and his hands search for a moment on the table before finding his glasses and replacing them to his face.

"Lucian is a real consequence man." Zara says and rubs him affectionately on the shoulder. "The real deal."

"When you hit a certain point, it's pretty easy to not give two shades of a fuck." He says and rests his hands on the lip of the table and returns to playing statue. I drink my coffee and try not to think about empty leather dry eye sockets. The waitress comes back over to our booth and asks us if we're ready to order yet and Zara sends her away with a request for more coffee. The phone on the table starts to vibrate and Zara picks it up saying, "This'll be him." And answering it; "Hello... Yeah... yeah we're here, same place... Booth at the back... Okay, see you soon." She replaces the phone onto the table.

"He's just parking up, he'll be here in two minutes." She says and Lucian says nothing.

"So you're taking drugs over the border?" I ask, trying to sound as nonchalant as possible.

"It's a soft border here." Zara explains, "And nobody really gives a shit about an old blind man and his carer."

The front door of Café Tropical opens and a short, dumpy looking Chinese man enters the restaurant, his eyes scanning around the tables and booths until he sees us and he puts his hand up and Zara waves back, nudging Lucian who says, "About time." The Chinese guy walks over looking me over with cautious eyes.

"He's fine." Zara says," he's with me." He nods at me, sits down and extends his hand saying. "I'm Sean."

"How's it going?"

"It's going good. Lucian, how are you?"

"I'm scratchy." He says, "I hope you're not expecting to eat lunch here."

"No, I know the drill." Sean says and leans back in his chair. "I'm good to go whenever you are."

Zara catches the eye of our waitress who is standing talking to somebody who looks like her boss and she comes back over to us. "Are you ready to order?"

"No, we just want the bill please." Zara gives her the cute girl smile with an edge of taking the piss and the waitress just absorbs it and says "Sure, no problem."

When we're all squared up we leave the restaurant, Zara putting on her thick woollen gloves before lightly guiding Lucian at his elbow, Sean and I walking behind.

"You're a Brit?" Sean asks as we step back out into the harsh stinging breeze.

"Afraid so." I roll the collar of my jacket up in some token effort of insulation.

"What happened to your face?"

"I walked into a door."

We walk a couple of blocks away from the Falls and Sean leads us into a parking lot where a Volvo defined by its ordinariness sits crookedly parked towards the back of the lot.

"Well, this is where we part ways." Zara says and Lucian runs his hand across the side bodywork until he locates the passenger door handle. Sean double presses a button on his keys and the central locking clunks open. Lucian gets in without saying anything. Sean opens the driver's door and leans on it looking at Zara.

"How are things with Colby?"

"Colby is doing just fine. Getting quite a movement developing across the other side."

"Yeah, I bet he is. You guys are something else that's for sure. Anyway," he says, "Nice to meet you." To me and "I'll see you when I see you Zara." She moves towards and gives him a kiss on the cheek and says "Look after my man."

"Always do." Sean says and tips a salute at her before getting in and closing the door. We step away from the car and I light a cigarette.

"He doesn't look much like a junk dealer." I say and Zara laughs.

"He's not. He just does the donkey work. Good money for what he does." We watch the Volvo pull out of the lot and disappear into the slow moving traffic.

"What happened to Lucian's eyes?" I ask her.

"He told you; he used to gamble a lot. When you mix in the circles that he has mixed in there is value in everything."

"He gambled his fucking eyes?" I shake my head at the madness of it.

"He's eight nine years old. He's seen enough." I'm beginning to think that Colby Stein and his people are not only fundamentally different in their attitudes but of a completely separate species altogether.

"Well, what now?" I say.

"Have you ever driven a left hand drive?"

"No."

"Do you want to?" And she walks over to bronze coloured Buick and slaps it on the roof.

"Sure. Why not?"

She giggles in that way of hers which I'm starting find even more attractive the more I hear it. "Here you go." She tosses the keys over to me and I fumble them into the door.

My orientation is totally thrown. I used to drive before it became too expensive to run a car but that was your standard British right hander. Sitting behind the steering wheel on the left of the car made no sense but in true consequence man style I decided to take the shot just for the hell of it. Zara climbs in next to me.

"Feels weird, huh? Ewan said it took him a good week to get used to your British cars."

"It feels very weird." I agree with her as I twist the key in the ignition and the car rumbles to life.

"No stick shift either." Zara says as I pull the lever into the R for reverse. Even looking over my right shoulder to check for moving vehicles or pedestrians feels strange. I jerkily reverse out of the space and clunk it back into drive and start to tentatively drive us around the parking lot.

"You're a natural." She says laughing and fiddling with the stereo.

"Where are we going to go?" I ask, my sense of direction totally shot.

"How about the casino?"

CHAPTER EIGHTEEN

The carpet is thick and plush here and all around people are in action. Old ladies sitting at the slots, rolling in dollar after dollar, chasing the dream. A knuckle of old boys are sitting round one of the blackjack tables, most of them wearing baseball caps with Niagara Falls emblazoned across the fronts, nobody seems to be winning much. Maybe that isn't the point when you hit retirement age. Maybe the point is to just be somewhere surrounded by other people and have the excuse of an activity.

The drive through town had been hazardous but by the time we pulled into the Niagara Casino I felt confident enough to reverse park into a space between a big black truck and a big red SUV with smoked out windows.

I have never caught the buzz of gambling, not even the scratch cards that promise you thousands of pounds a year for the rest of your life for the price of a Coke. People get hooked on the chance of it. The ever luminous chance of something for nothing, or at least for not very much; everybody is greedy for something.

Nobody hangs out in a casino at Niagara Falls in the middle of the day for a good time. There is a definite supply and demand of a need going on in here. Little thin haired ladies sit all hunched up over the slots with stringy blue veins hanging out from under their chins their dribble collecting in the cups that they pull quarters from. Twenty four hour junky dudes in dark glasses with sweat patches at the armpits of their suit jackets crack their knuckles and jabber edgily over double Vodka Screwdrivers.

"Three big down." One guy says.

"Two and a half up." Says another one sitting next to him, both of them look burnt out and frazzled. As far as I can tell they're the same person. And they're all over the place; these little blue ladies and burnt out fat men with receding hairlines and sweaty top lips. Instant wealth and easy luxury, these are the dreams that we are supposed to be chasing. What else is there?

I feel lightheaded and I'm pretty sure that they drug the air conditioning in the same way as they do in Megamarket. Maybe that's what turns all the old ladies blue? We walk through the guts of the casino and it feels like the apocalypse.

At the bar we order dirty martinis and sit there with the air conditioning blowing at our faces. A man with sand coloured hair and a white tuxedo comes over and props himself on the bar next to us. His eyes are puffy and pinched closed in a permanent squint.

"Jack and Coke." He mumbles and nobody pays him any attention. "Jack and Coke." He says louder. "Jack and fucking Coke." Eventually an obedient looking barman comes over.

"Yes sir?"

"Jesus Christ. Jack and Coke." He coughs into his sleeve and I see that he has blood on his cuff.

Strawberries and cream.

"So," He says turning to us, leaning on his elbow. "How are you folks enjoying Niagara Falls?" Just like we're old friends.

"It's okay." Zara and I say at the same time.

"Shit, it's boring as hell down here." He says and takes a drink, slamming his glass back down on the bar, rattling the ice. He wipes his hand down the front of his jacket and extends it out to Zara. "Reeve Evett." He says and Zara shakes his hand. "What are you two doing here?"

"Just having a look around, you know, checking it out." I say shaking his hand.

"Well, it's boring as hell down here." He says. "You need to see the shit that's going on upstairs?"

"What's upstairs?" Zara asks.

"The Sky Lounge."

"That sounds cool."

"Jesus. You have no idea." And he knocks the rest of his drink back and slides the glass up the bar. "You ever heard of the Evett watch?"

"What?"

"The Evett watch." He says wiping his sleeve over his mouth and then squishing his lips together.

"No."

"I didn't think so." He says digging his hand into his jacket pocket. "That's why I'm here." He pulls out a square black box and sets it on the bar in front of us. "Take a look."

"You're here because of a watch?" I say not too sure what to make of this guy in the white tuxedo with the blood on his sleeve.

"No, I'm here because you've never heard of the Evett watch." He opens the box and sits back admiring what's inside. "There she is." He says with a parent's mix of pride and sadness. Inside is a smart looking digital wristwatch with a liquid smooth screen. "You can operate up to five hundred different functions on that baby." He says and he looks at us with his puffy purple eyes. He has those red and blotchy cheeks of an alcoholic, that splatter of exploded blood vessels.

"Looks good." I say. "What's the story?"

"I was about ten minutes away from Apple buying this beauty from me, straight up. Eight million or there abouts. You can open the garage door with that."

"What happened?" Zara asks all wide eyed tell me more.

"Shop on the internet. Watch porn. Pretty cool." He coughs and winces and bangs his hand down on the bar making the watch box jump.

"What happened?" Zara asks again.

"I invented that fucker, all on my own. Not me and a bunch of engineers and technicians and what have you. Me. Just me. Night after night, over a year in my workshop."

"And..."

"Programmed it; up to five hundred functions in there. Apart from it doesn't tell the fucking time."

"What?"

"It's a watch that does everything apart from tell the time." And Reeve sighs and he runs his hand over his hair and for a moment he looks like he's going to cry. He holds his hand out with his thumb and index finger a quarter of an inch apart. "This close." He says.

"You made a watch that doesn't tell the time?"

"I guess I got carried away." He shakes his head and puts his hand up to catch the barman's attention. The barman comes over. Reeve orders a Jack and coke. "So anyway, they took my design, made it tell the time and boom. Here I am."

"Can't you take them to court or something?" Zara asks as the barman puts another drink in front of him.

"Well, shit. Why would I do that?"

"Because they stole your watch."

"Nah, fuck that. You don't beat guys like that. And anyway gives me an excuse to drink. Gives me an excuse to come here." He knocks back half of his glass and then squints at us. "There was an element of payoff." And he winks. "You ever heard of an end of the world party?"

"No."

"No."

"Well, shit. You've got to come upstairs with me. Some freaks up there I tell ya." He finishes off his drink and stands up and his tuxedo jacket uncrumples around him. "Come on." He says putting the watch back into his pocket. Zara looks at me and I shrug.

We walk with Reeve between banks of slot machines towards the elevator

He presses the button at the top of the column and the doors shut behind us closing us inside a mirrored box. He slouches back against the rail and watches as numbers tick by on the digital display.

Reflections of reflections.

Infinite Stacker.

The doors ping open onto a deserted corridor with thick carpet the colour of blood.

"This way." Roger says leading us down the corridor and round the corner and onward. We go around another corner, Reeve muttering something about freaks and madness.

Up ahead a heavyset bouncer dressed all in black stands guard in front of a plain looking door.

"Who are they?" He demands taking a step forward.

"Relax Charlie, it's all good man." Reeve says clapping the bouncer on the shoulder.

"I've told you about this before." The bouncer says shaking his head. "The big suits don't like it."

"Yeah, well. Come on man, last time. I promise." With that drunken grin. The bouncer opens the door shaking his head. Reeve claps him on the shoulder, grabs him by the face and smacks a kiss on his cheek. He turns round and walks backwards through the door and says. "Welcome to the end of the world."

Madness.

At every angle there is madness.

You hear it before your eyes realise what they're seeing.

Reeve gives a maniac's laugh and looks around gleefully. There are people everywhere and everybody looks wasted. The place looks like a fucked up carnival. There are people in costumes and masks swinging around deliriously as a scrappy Jazz combo rips through some mad sped up tune. The Sky Lounge is a big private bar with floor to ceiling windows all along the far side looking out over Niagara Falls and the crisp afternoon that surrounds it but nobody is here for the view. A clown sits at the bar with his head in his hands whilst a ballet dancer rubs his curly orange hair.

Tuxedos in various states of disrepair stagger around arm in arm.

Right next to us, next to the door which closes behind us, is a full height cage of brass bars stretching out to the corner of the room. Inside it there are parrots and toucans squawking and jabbering. A couple of flamingos five foot tall strut about in the shallow water. Like somebody has grabbed a chunk of jungle, greenery and all and dropped it whole into the cage.

The air is hot and wet.

The Sky Lounge is a living thing.

Another clown walks by in front of us juggling swords. Somebody else is breathing fire. Another guy in a white tux bear hugs Reeve and sticks a fat cigar in his mouth. Out of the corner of my eye I see Zara slowly look around the room, taking it all in.

I've never seen anything like it.

Reeve turns back to us and takes the cigar out of his mouth and looks like he's about to say something but in the next moment he is knocked sideways by two half naked men made out of solid muscle and wearing boxing gloves as they batter each other, neither raising any defence. Reeve gets up laughing and applauds the fighters as strings of blood and spit hang from their mouths and noses.

"Look at them go." He screams above the noise. "Shit, now that is boxing." And he jumps up and down throwing a few shadow punches of his own. "Let's get a drink." He says wiping sweat off his face.

"What's going on?" I shout.

"What?"

"What's going on?"

"It's the end of the world party. Let's get a drink." And he gestures towards the bar and leads us deeper into the Sky Lounge.

We cross the room, through the sweaty crush of bodies of both the bloated and the exotic type trying to look in all directions at once.

The bar is armed by three girls in bikinis and three guys in speedos, all of them California brown and toned all of them with smiles so white and wide that they must be stuck on. Reeve screams one over, a blonde in a green bikini. He cups his hands over her ear and shouts something. The girl, never dropping the smile, nods her head and goes away to the fridge at the back of the bar. The band closes down the tune and then immediately starts up a frantic waltz.

"Why is it called the end of the world party?" I ask close up at Reeve's ear.

"People get the fear. They want to party." He shouts back. "They've been having them every now and again since nine eleven."

"Really?"

"Shit man, I don't know, people are nuts." He shrugs his shoulders. The blonde in the green bikini comes back to us with a bottle of Champagne in a silver bucket filled with ice. She places three glasses in front of us. "Get the glasses." Reeve shouts at Zara as he picks up the bucket. "Let's go outside."

He leads us again through the room, now towards the balcony. We weave our way across the sticky wooden floor between spinning bodies and flailing limbs.

Reeve shuts the glass door behind us and suddenly it's quiet. There are clusters of people up and down the balcony, sitting at tables of standing around smoking. Somebody is sitting cross legged staring out between the rails banging out a slow metronome beat on a pair of bongos. A cowboy wearing only a pair of jeans and a hat is lying back on a lounger surrounded by people all full of giggles and hushed chatter. When I look closer I can see that the people around him are pressing burning cigarettes onto his body.

"What the fuck?" I say.

"What?" Reeve asks looking around. "Oh." He says as he follows my gaze. "Tony, what the shit man?" He shouts at the cowboy. Tony looks up and winces.

"Hey Reeve man." The cowboy grins and then grimaces as another cigarette stabs home.

"What the fuck are you doing man?"

"It's the constellations." He says. "Check it out." He stands up and stretches himself into the shape of a cross.

"We're making him a map of the stars." Says a girl sucking on a lollypop.

"Well, shit." Reeve shrugs his shoulders. Down at the far end of the balcony there is a diving board that jumps into nothing.

"What's that?" Zara says.

"Sometimes it gets too much for some. They take a jump." Reeve shakes his head. "I told you these people are nuts."

"How is this allowed to happen?" I ask.

"Money. Shit, it's all about money."

"Who are these people?"

"Rich people, crazy people. People waiting for the end of the world." Reeve pours Champagne into the three glasses and raises his. "A toast," He says. "To the end of the world." And we all clink glasses and drink.

The afternoon becomes the evening in a blur of colours and drinks. And in a heart blink we're on the cusp of midnight. The band that has been playing almost non-stop since we arrived quietens down and everybody hushes and gathers around the Sky Lounge and watches the massive clock at the end of the room.

"Ten." Somebody shouts and then everybody else joins in the count down.

"Nine." Reeve is wasted hanging off our shoulders with a vacant grin.

"Eight." Like the last days of Rome.

"Seven." Like when the Third Reich fell.

"Six."

"Five."

"Four." In the cage the Flamingos have pulled a leg up and have fallen asleep.

"Three."

"Two." Everything is cranked up.

"One." A micro second pause, a collective intake of breath.

"Happy new day."

A complete lack of understanding.

CHAPTER NINETEEN

We spill out of the elevator onto the roof level of the parking garage, over the town of Niagara somewhere to the east the first blossoms of sunlight are breaking through the night.

"That was fucked up." I say and shiver as a cold wind blows across us.

"It sure was." Says Zara and then she wheels round in front of me and takes my hands in her gloved ones and stands up on tiptoes and kisses me.

"What was that for?" I ask when she pulls back.

"Nothing. Just because." And she kisses me again. I haven't kissed a girl since Lucy.

We walk hand in hand towards the edge of the roof and for a few moments we just stand there looking out over the sunrise and it doesn't matter how much craziness there is in the world. Eventually we head back to the car.

"What now?" Zara says as she settles into the driver's seat and pulls the door closed behind her.

"I need to think about going home." I say and my voice seems faraway and detached as if it belongs to somebody else. I yawn and snap myself back into the present.

"Have you booked a plane?"

"No, I'm just going to hope for the best."

"Consequence man." She says and laughs a little. "You want to go and get some breakfast first?"

"Sure." I say suddenly realising that I can't remember the last time I ate anything. Zara fires up the engine and reverses.

"There's this sweet little diner on the edge of town." She says and we begin to wind our way down the levels.

I make Zara stop at Niagara Central station and I run inside and collect my bag. At this time of day the station is nearly deserted, just a few guys in suits making the early morning commute to Toronto or wherever. Some skinny dude with dark circles under his eyes and an orange vest is picking up the litter and the remains of a thousand takeaway sandwiches an army of pigeons and crows surround him fighting for scraps. I head over to my locker and insert the key.

A gust of wind booms around the high up beams and the birds take flight in a flurry of squawks and fast moving feathers. All except for one which just carries on hopping around, its broken wing flopping weakly as it scuttles around the red metal benches too distressed to even scavenge.

Slinging my bag over my shoulder I shut the locker and turn around, the damaged bird slows its frantic shudders and just kind of stands there breathing heavily and silently and suddenly our eyes meet. I stand there for a moment just staring at it and it feels as if there is some meaning in it, hidden but somehow pressing against me but in a beat my stomach groans and I realise that I'm starving and I walk out of the station without looking back.

At the edge of Niagara Zara pulls into a twenty four diner too tired to remember its own name. We walk across the cracked concrete of the parking lot and Zara pulls her gloves off and folds them into her pocket. I hold the door like a gentleman.

We sit down at opposites at a booth with red plastic seats and a sad window view. Across the floor a family of four are reading menus and bickering. Dad is wearing a baseball cap and mum is trying to organise the sister and her younger brother who is more interested in drawing faces with the sugar.

"Oh, to be a kid again." Zara says shaking her head and pulling a menu out of the rack.

"You can say that again." I say. Cromer pier in the rain and all of those things. Clinging, shrinking memories of everything I've ever known across the other side of the world and my shoulders sag a bit.

"Are you alright?" Zara asks.

"Me? Yeah, I'm fine. Just thinking that's all."

"What you thinking about?"

"Just thinking." I say and smile. "What's next for you?"

"I don't know." She says, "I don't really plan ahead, it's the way I was brought up I suppose."

A waitress with an all-night face comes over to the table and opens her pad.

"You guys ready to order?" She asks. I order a big plate of bacon and eggs and Zara orders French toast, we both order black coffees. Another waitress with plates of food balanced up her arms goes to the table where the family are sitting and sets them down and the kids immediately stop fooling around.

Outside the sky is pale blue and pure and all the bother in the world seems very petty and faraway.

"Don't you want to do something other than stack shelves?" Zara asks as the waitress puts cups of coffee in front of us. I rip the tops off of two sachets of brown sugar and twist them into my cup.

"Like what?" I ask.

"I don't know. Just something else."

"I don't know what else I can do." I say. It's like anything, if you do it long enough you forget what it's like to not do it. It becomes a part of you, it becomes all of you. I am Stacker and blah blah blah. You become institutionalised in a way.

"You don't seem like you enjoy it very much." She says.

"I don't really." I say and look out the window, home seems very far away.

"You should join up with my dad." She says. "He can help you."

"I'm not sure I'm that kind of person. I think I'm beyond help."

"That's what he does. He shows people another way. He helps people; he says nobody is beyond help. It's just conditioning." It's all just conditioning. Conditioning and diet, that's all you are, really. When it's all boiled down and the tallow separates from the fat, it's conditioning and diet and the songs you used to sing on the radio. But if you're not that you're nothing.

"I have family though. I can't do what you guys do." I say. "They wouldn't understand."

"Other people's expectations are a form of consequence." Zara says and for the first time I'm not sure if she knows what she is saying and inside of me I get that dropping feeling that estranged feeling of reality booming home.

We eat in quiet for a bit.

The family opposite finish up their meals and scrunch up their napkins. I watch them blankly as they settle their bill and get up to leave. A sudden sadness pushes through the windows and liquefies into condensation. I draw a smiley face.

When we've finished our food we pay up and leave. We light cigarettes on our way to the car. The family from inside are bickering again as they arrange themselves around a pale blue Volvo and the lights flash as the doors unlock and they all pile in. Through the thin spindles of shrubbery that divide the parking lot from the freeway I watch the traffic. I want to go home. Zara puts her gloves on and knots the scarf around her neck.

The Volvo pulls out of the parking lot and aims its nose forward. Just another family moving on, going to another place.

"You've gone quiet again." Zara says as we get into the car and sit there smoking with the doors open.

"I'm alright." I say and look at my cigarette. I don't feel alright though. There's some feeling of desperation or something like that scratching around at the top of my stomach. Like I know something is going to go wrong. But then a voice in my head tells me that things have already gone wrong.

Relax, enjoy the ride.

The sky is the same colour as the road as we peel away from the diner. I slump back in my chair and watch the traffic.

"I'm tired." Zara says. Up ahead the traffic builds up, snarls up and slows. We slow down with it. I'm thinking about traffic jams on the way to the coast.

"Fuck this." Zara says. "I'm too tired for this." She aims the car onto the shoulder of the road and accelerates smoothly.

"What are you doing?" I ask her alarmed.

"Our turnoff is only a half mile away."

Apparently pigeon's eyes have a slow shutter speed. That's why when you drive towards them they don't know what's going on until the last second. Like living in a constant strobe light. They don't move until the last second, or until it's too late.

You see the sky merge with the road and the traffic.

You see a Volvo, the impression of pale blue. Nothing but a shape.

Your hand grabs at the door as your body tenses up. Your foot stamps on an imaginary brake pedal.

Straddling the lines and looking like trouble.

Zara hits the brakes and the car locks up and I brace myself. But the car realigns itself and for a moment I think everything is going to be alright. The car half on the shoulder, half chewing up turf.

You see a little boy, maybe seven or eight at the open backdoor.

You see him look up and you see his eyes not understanding what is about to happen. A whole lifetime of potential receding in a heartbeat.

You see him realise and he starts to run in that little boy way, all puffed out cheeks and clenched chubby hands on the end of short arm pistons. Trying to get out of the way.

This is what horror looks like.

The car hits him and he flies up in the air like a ragdoll with his arms and legs flapping against the sky and he lands heavily in a heap. We stop sharply with smoke from the tires rising up around us in purple ribbons. Somebody screams and in the rear-view mirror his mum runs to him and cradles him.

Like living in a strobe light.

Zara twists around in her seat her eyes wide and bright white and she screams something. Behind us dad is kneeling down by his wife, by his kid. The boys sister stands on the verge with all colour drained from her face.

Up ahead our turnoff, beside us choked up traffic. I look at Zara and she looks at me. And then she's driving, accelerating hard down the shoulder.

"You can't..." I say. "We have to go back." I scream at her but she's not even there and I don't know what to do.

Everything is shrinking.

Zara slices back onto the road, cutting up some orange pickup that leans on the horn and then we're gone, moving across the breadth of the road, into the fast lane. Forward at pace.

It could all be a dream I suppose.

That nasty feeling of dread.

CHAPTER TWENTY

Just silence until the airport.
Pulling up at the terminal Zara says it's just a manmade thing.
I don't say anything. I grab my bag and shut the door. I don't say anything.
I book a flight from a blonde with lipstick on her teeth. Five hours to wait. To kill.
Sitting on plastic airport seats and not talking to anyone.
I go outside and smoke cigarettes until they're all gone.
Eventually I board the plane and everybody is smiling apart from me. I've forgotten how.
Cutting through clouds and rattling turbulence.
Like I'm stoned on something, just dazed.
Somebody asks me if I'd like a drink. I try and sleep.
The sky is the colour of Volvos.

CHAPTER TWENTY ONE

I've been wandering along this beach for hours now. Occasionally I'll stop and look out over handwritten waves towards the long flat ships Morse coded along the horizon. The day is hot and the sun is blazing at near enough its highest point. Sweat drips down my face and evaporates before it reaches my neck.

I'm carrying a few things in a Megamarket carrier bag. A bottle of water which I had previously frozen but which is now completely thawed. A vinyl copy of Bob Dylan's Greatest Hits, my father's Swiss Army knife and a Princess Diana ten year anniversary mug.

The beach that I'm on is wide and golden and almost completely free of pebbles and shale. I decide to take off my shoes so I sit down and pull them off in turn, looping their laces together and putting them into the bag. Whilst I think about it I take a long drink of the now tepid water. I'm briefly concerned about the water beading on the outside of the bottle, warping or damaging in some way beyond my understanding the Bob Dylan record. But I replace it nonetheless. I stand up and fumble in the pocket of my jeans for my cigarettes. Distressingly it seems that I have lost my lighter. I continue to pat down my pockets just because it seems like the right thing to do. Nothing. Not there. I even rummage through my bag even though I know that it won't be there. The sea is as flat as a mirror and the horizon so stretched and wide that it appears that the ships aren't moving at all.

What I wouldn't give to be working for the airport cigarette lighter collectors right now.

Still, the day is beautiful, the sky a perfect unblemished blue. Tucking the cigarette behind my ear I look around. The beach is completely deserted. Deserted except for in the distance. Squinting and shading my eyes against the sun I make out that there is solitary figure walking towards me, I think, maybe at five hundred yards, nothing more than a thin black smudge but I suppose that's what we all are at that distance. Sighing to myself as my sweat soaks into the cigarette and my damp hair curls against it I walk back the way I came towards the lone figure.

We are maybe one hundred meters apart and I can make out that the figure is a man of maybe my age. I wave to him and after a cautious delay he waves back.

"Hello." I call out to him and drop the bag down at my feet where it settles into the golden sands.

"Hello." The man calls back, "Lovely day for a walk isn't it?"

"It certainly is." The closer he approaches the less we shout. "I was wondering if you possibly have a cigarette lighter on you."

"What's that?"

"Maybe some matches?"

"What matches?" He calls back in a puzzled tone. He's closer now I can make out his features. He is taller than me, skinny too. His hair is long and dark and hangs about his face where it seems to mingle with his thick dark beard. He is wearing denim cut-offs and his checked shirt is open. One of his hands is in its pocket and the other one; strangely enough is carrying a Megamarket carrier bag.

"I've lost my lighter." I say running my hands through my hair and inadvertently knocking the cigarette from behind my ear and it falls to the ground and seems to disappear. "I've lost my lighter." I say again looking around for my smoke.

"Man, all I've got are matches." Says the man and shows me the inside of his bag. Sure enough his bag is stuffed full with box upon box of matches all colliding crazily like Lego blocks. "Help yourself." And he nods at me.

"Thank you." I say and pull out a box of matches, proper matches, not those safety ones that you give to kids to play with. I crouch down next to my own bag and brush at the sand around it looking for my cigarette.

"You lost something buddy?"

"I've lost my cigarette."

"Lovely day for a walk." He says again looking down at me. "Hot though." He drops his bag down next to mine and sits down brushing his hands round behind him and leaning back and looking out to sea. He looks familiar; there is something half remembered around his eyes. I give up looking for my cigarette and sit down myself letting the hot sand run over my knuckles. The beach doesn't look as wide anymore, as if the tide has stealthily moved in unnoticed.

"I needed to clear my head." Says the man before I have even asked him why he looks so sad. He begins drawing circles in the sand with his finger.

"Why?" I ask, still vaguely looking for my lost cigarette.

"Because I'm one of three and it can be a bit of a drag."

"One of three? Brothers and sisters?"

"We're triplets." He says, "Identical triplets. It's hard to be an individual when there are other people who look exactly like you and think in the same way."

"I can imagine." I say thinking about it. "How do you know which is which?"

"I don't most of the time. That's why I carry the matches."

"I see." I don't really see and as if he can tell he says;

"I'm the one with the matches."

"I see." I say again slightly puzzled. "What do the others carry?"
He looks surprised for a moment before looking up slowly at me and saying. "I don't know. I can't remember."

"Well, I don't suppose it's that important if you can't remember." And I slap him on the back cheerfully.

"I guess." He says doubtfully and looks back out to sea.

The tide is nearly at our feet now and yet I feel no need to move back or even move at all. Curious about the cigarette though.

"What have you got in your bag?" He asks and I take out the Bob Dylan record, the Swiss Army knife, the Princess Diana mug and the dripping bottle of water and line them up on the sand between my feet and the sea.

"Are you a triplet as well?"

"No, I have an older brother but we don't look the same."

"Why do you carry those things?"

"I don't know. I suppose you have to carry something's with you, just in case."

I pick up my things and put them back in the bag just before the sea begins to lap at our toes. I put the bag behind me as the water reaches my shins. I don't even think about moving.

"Do you shop at Megamarket?" I ask him looking at his bag as he puts it on his lap.

"Doesn't everybody? I work there too."

"So do I." I say completely unsurprised. "Do you enjoy it?"

"No, not really; it's worse than being a triplet. I get in trouble a lot."

The sea has really caught up with us now and I can feel it painting me cold. For some reason I decide to lie down. Just at that moment an alarm clock washes up right close to my face and rings rudely in my ear.

I wake up in a cold sweat and silence my phone alarm. Six thirty Monday morning. All over the country people are waking up and hating their jobs and hating themselves.

The letter from Donny Brinklow had come through with the usual overdraft statements and junk mail. I had only opened it because even the envelope said Megamarket. I was again *invited* to attend another meeting with him and again I was *invited* to move my shift to an eight five standard. Today feels like nothing more than an echo. I reach blindly across my bedside table and find my cigarettes and sit up and smoke, giving my body and mind a precious few moments to align themselves with the day. I use the pint glass next to my bed as an ashtray. For some reason I'm thinking about my brother.

Without realising it I have walked to the bathroom and stood underneath the tepid, weak jets of water. I close my eyes and turn my face up to the shower head and all of a sudden I remember Canada and my body lurches at the force of a car hitting a child and I stagger back, nearly falling along the bottom of the bath. I slowly bend my knees and rest my hands on the edges of the bath and lower my head. Out of the water the air is cold and I'm shaking and when I open my eyes I see lines of goose bumps boiling up along my arms.

I throw up.

Brown and yellow liquid accented with chunks of orange and a foamy cream colour spill from my mouth and traces its way through my legs towards the plughole. I close my eyes but all I can see is a broken child's body with its limbs at all the wrong angles. I throw up until I'm dry heaving and my throat feels shredded.

I watch the world out the window of the bus as the first spill of morning light moans through the overcast sky. I'm feeling pretty vacant and could do with a drink.

Jesus Christ.

Is this what becomes of the doomed? Sitting on a damp, stinking bus watching the world judder backwards in its shades of grey and endless red lights. I used to think I lived in such a beautiful town.

If you look close enough and I mean closer than you thought was even possible you can see it; some giant wave of something nameless engulfing this whole bus. I can see it seeping through the windows and condensing upon them. And everybody suffers from it. There is no escape. We pull into some nowhere bus stop with the indicator clicking like a metronome. Outside a line of people, all hunched shoulders and heads down in collars begins to file on board. I watch them without looking. Suddenly my eye is caught by a man standing at the back of the line, he's all dressed in black and I can't see any of the features of his face, obscured as they are by the gloom of the morning. I know he sees me though and a fist of paranoia tightens around my chest. The line-up shuffles on board but this guy in black doesn't move, he just stands. And he watches.

Back in the traffic and I put the strange shadow man to the back of mind and look out at the familiar streets as they snarl up and jam in every direction. An old man walking with a stick wobbles up the bus and sits down next to me making me bunch up my coat and shuffle closer to the window. He mutters something that sounds like good morning but I don't bother answering.

The bus crawls past my old college and all those sixteen to eighteen year olds strutting in dressed in the latest fashion full of fresh faced optimism and good times. Good luck to the fuckers I think before sadly realising that my time at college was the happiest time of my life and that was half a life time ago.

Even that didn't get off to the best of starts.

CHAPTER TWENTY TWO

Me and Mike stood around the smoking area just taking it all in. First day of college and Mike had already got some girl's phone number. I was still getting used to not wearing a uniform and being allowed to smoke openly. Over in the corner, by the treeline some pasty kids with attention hair had just fired up a joint. This was lunchtime at college.

"Man, this is what it is about." Mike said. "Freedom." He clapped his hands together and laughed.

"How's your morning been?" I asked.

"Just a load of induction bullshit; easy living." Everywhere you looked there was optimism; you could see it shimmering in the bright September air. Everybody looked happy.

"Who is this girl then?" I asked as I twisted out my cigarette in the sand of the plant pot ashtray.

"Girl called Helen, from across town. We have Business together." Mike kept looking around, his eyes flittering from group to group. "There are a lot of girls here." He said. "Beats the shit out of school."

"That it does."

"You know what we should do?"

"No, what?"

"We should go for a drink." I could see that glint of mischief in his eye.

"Now?"

"Sure, why not?" And he clapped me on the shoulder and said. "There's a bar just down the road. My brother says everyone goes there."

"Sure, why the fuck not?"

We walked back across the college site with our bags slung over our slouching shoulders. A window cleaner was halfway up his ladder wiping off the large panes of the main hall. We both ducked under it just for the hell of it. We crossed the large square in the centre of the site which was known as the Quad for obvious reasons and carried on through the canteen. A dude in a Nirvana T shirt sat cross legged on a table riffing some twelve bar on an acoustic guitar while a group around him chatted shit and ate burgers.

We crossed the car park passing between teacher's cars and onto a path well worn down by years and years of lunchtime student drinkers. We crossed the main road outside the college and turned right heading towards town.

"These are going to be the best years of our life." Mike said as we walked. "Need to make the most of them."

Cody's was a low slung beat up place set a little way back from the road, separated from the pavement by a rough parking area of puckered concrete with half a dozen picnic benches scattered about in front of it.

Inside the air was thick and blue with smoke and the place was packed out with brazenly underage drinkers. The Pogues blasted out of the Juke box and the clack of pool balls rattling together cut through the dull babble of voices. We immediately felt comfortable.

"What are you drinking?" I asked Mike as we got to the bar and dumped our bags at our feet.

"Snakebite and black."

"What the fuck is snakebite?"

"Half a lager, half a cider and a squirt of blackcurrant. Trust me." Mike winked. "My brother drinks it all the time at Uni. Says it gets him right fucked up."

The barman looked up from his newspaper and rolled his eyes as he came over.

"Yeah." He said, his T shirt barely stretched over his stomach, his tattooed arms looked like weathered rope. I could feel my pulse in my neck, as adrenaline dumped into my blood.

"Two Snakebite and blacks." I said with as much gravitas as I could muster. He looked at me and said. "You got any ID?"

"I left it at home." I said and met his eyes without blinking. He gazed back at me and I could feel Mike's foot nervously tapping against his bag on the floor.

"Sure you did." He said and shook his head. "Whatever. Two snakebite and blacks, seven pound eighty." I handed over my money and felt a sudden surge of boundless euphoria. This was it. This was what life was about. Drinking in pubs and hanging out with mates and not having a care in the whole world. This was it alright. This was freedom.

We sat down on a small table in the corner and for a few moments neither of us spoke. We just looked around, taking it all in. Everybody looked the same but different, everybody lit up by some magic flush of optimism and youth.

"This is the start of our lives, man." I said shaking my head. "It's just beginning."

"I'll drink to that." And we clinked our glasses together and drank and lit up cigarettes and laughed.

Three pints and an hour and a half later we left Cody's and headed back to college. We arrived back halfway through fourth period when I was supposed to be in my Film Studies induction and Mike was supposed to be in Economics. It didn't seem to matter, plenty of others had skipped out on it and we all sat around in the canteen drinking Cokes with our feet on the tables feeling light headed like we owned the world.

I sat down at the back of the classroom and tried to pay attention. Outside across the playing fields a flock of birds was pecking around the rugby pitch. There wasn't a cloud in the sky and the sun hung there in on its mid-afternoon plain and the whole world seemed calm. The last induction class was English Literature, my favourite subject; I had got into college partially on the back of my double A grade in English Literature and Language. It's what I wanted to study at University. Outside a lone airplane cut a white trail across the sky, a gust of wind fluttered the trees around the perimeter of the field; the birds took flight with one mind.

"Are you even listening?" It took a moment to realise that the teacher was talking to me.

"Yes Miss." I said as I blinked the room back into focus.

"Don't call me Miss; you're not at school now. You're at college now and we expect mature attention spans."

"Yes Carol." I said and rubbed the back of my neck.

"As I was saying, your success in this subject depends on you having a certain amount of passion for English Literature. Do you have that passion?"

"Yeah, I guess I do."

"You guess? Who's your favourite author?"

"Kafka." I said without hesitation. That sense of bewilderment, that unknowable feeling of dread. Carol looked at me and nodded gently and gave a small smile.

"And what is it that you like about Kafka's work?" She asked and I could hear the girl sat in front of me turn to her neighbour and whisper "Who's Kafka?"

"Well," I began, "I like his confusion and I like his style."

"What do you mean his confusion?"

"The world he describes, it's disorientating, and nothing quite makes sense." I said, I felt my mouth getting dry and my cheeks felt warm and I wondered if I had given the wrong answer. I wondered when the questions would stop.

"So you think that all his story's take place in the same world?"

"Yes."

"And it is these worlds that the author creates that are what drives the subject of English Literature." Carol said, finally addressing the class in general again.

I didn't look out of the window for the rest of the class.

I met Mike at the bus stop and we leant against the wall and smoked cigarettes as we waited for the number seven. My phone shrieked out its text message tone and I pulled it out of my pocket just as the bus swung into view.

"There is no way that I am going to spend the next two years waiting for late buses." Mike said hauling his bag up onto his shoulder. "The sooner I start driving the better."

I opened the message on my phone, it was from Rob. "Turn on the news." I put my phone back into my pocket and picked up my own bag as the bus wheezed to a stop in front of us and we filed on.

"I liked that bar." Mike said as we sat down halfway down the top deck. "I think we'll spend a lot of time there."

"You reckon?"

"Yes I do." Mike said and settled back in his seat and watched the world go by outside.

We got off at the same stop and Mike turned right and I turned left and walked the last hundred odd meters at a leisurely pace, letting the experiences of the day settle. It was quiet; nobody walking the pavement, no cars, no noise, nothing.

As soon as I pulled the front door shut behind me I knew something was wrong. The television was on in the living room and the television was never on until after we had eaten dinner, daytime television, my mum said, would ruin my generation.

"Mum…" I called out, dumping my bag at the foot of the stairs.

"I'm in here sweetheart. Have you heard?" I could tell by the strain in her voice that something was up.

"Heard what? What are you talking about?" I said kicking my shoes off and then standing in the doorway I saw it for the first time.

Pure blue sky.

Two towers spewing black smoke.

"Shit."

"They hijacked some planes." My mum said looking at me like I was the first thing she'd seen that wasn't on television. Streaming red ticker tape ran across the bottom of the screen full of word like attack and devastation and history. I sat down on the sofa my eyes locked on the images. Cameras rolled on the streets of New York the whole place covered in ash and debris. Replayed footage of a plane that looked so tiny in the context of the sky smashing into the World Trade Centre and exploding into violent fire and smoke.

Over and over.

And over and over.

Different angles and breathless analysis, everybody had something to say. Advertising executives somewhere had hit the jackpot. We were all characters in a movie now. We were all fiction.

I don't know how long we sat there and silently watched the same loops of footage with different arrangements of words spoken and overlaid over the top. And we watched on in silent horror as one by one the twin towers collapsed into themselves and fell in a crushing rumbling freefall with smoke and dust as thick as the screams were hysterical, rolling outward strangling everything in its path until the world was shadowed and the sky wasn't blue anymore.

"This is your Kennedy moment." My mum said eventually.

"My what?"

"That's what they used to say, 'where were you when Kennedy was shot?' that's what they used to say."

"I was at college." I said quietly, more to myself than to my mum. "My first day of college." And I knew then that the whole world had gone through some massive shift far beyond my comprehension. This was something defining.

"If there is a God then he's not on our side anymore."

"I didn't know he ever was."

"Or maybe he just left."

CHAPTER TWENTY THREE

I am Stacker and I hope there is a God so I have something to focus my anger on. This rage and hate that wells up inside of me and overspills out of my eyes and mouth into what I see and what I say. I would suicide bomb Heaven if I could make such a concept float.

"Milk." Demands the woman who has appeared in front me, she could be forty or she could be sixty, it doesn't matter. When they see the name badge, the apron and the charcoal tie they mostly drop the preamble of *Please could you show me...*

"Right this way." I don't give the pre-requisite smile and hope that nobody is watching the CCTV too closely. Megamarket policy is to show not tell. Like teaching a toddler to roll a joint. I lead the woman back up to the top of Soft Drinks, Mixers and Crisps and Left back towards the chilled Fresh Foods section. Right around the corner and Blam. She must've walked straight past the ten meter long run of one pint and two pint and four pint varieties of the red, blue and green tops, mostly green. She must've looked directly at it.

"Right here." I present the milk with a sweep of my hand. She must be wearing half a cow of makeup. Powders and pastes plastered into the crevices of her broad face. Her hair is stiff with hairspray.

"Thank you." She says but she doesn't mean it. I wander back to my cage, another tiny part of my soul snapped off.

The customers are the worst part of the job. This is why I work graveyard. I should be asleep right now.

I could be a journalist right now.

I could be a teacher.

I crouch down and prepare myself again to lift up another polythene wrapped bundle of two litre multipack Coke bottles off of the bottom shelf of the cage onto the fold down middle shelf of the cage. As I straighten up I see somebody standing at the top of my aisle watching me but when I look up they're gone. Customers moving up and down the aisles so practised it looks like they're on rails. In the future everything we do will be on rails with no missteps or deviations. Smooth and fluid.

The smoking area is busier during the days. Amanda sits on the bench saying "Oooh fuck ain't it cold." Every minute or so. Amanda dies on checkouts every day. She's worked here longer than me, there used to be a few of us back when I was on days, who would go out every payday and blast through a chunk of it in The Crown. I don't know where everybody else has gone but Amanda is still here.

"Oooh fuck, ain't it cold?" This time phrased as a question.

"Sure is."

"Are you back on days now? I saw you a couple of weeks ago.

"No still on nights."

"What you doing in on days then?" She sucks hard on her cigarette the orange ember growing long and tapering into a dart as it tends to do when you pull too hard on a cigarette.

"Got in a bit of bother with Sam, Donny Brinklow is investigating it."

"Oooh." Amanda throws the end of her cigarette into the yellow bucket of brown water where it hisses resentfully as she lights another. "What have you been up to? Haven't seen you about for ages." She says looking up at me.

"Oh, nothing much really, you know how it goes. Just existing." I say shrugging and throwing my cigarette away.

"Where's your name badge?" Amanda asks sounding genuinely shocked. I look down the front of myself to the top left hand corner of my apron where my name badge should be pinned.

"I don't know."

"You need to order another one."

At five to ten I take a piss and wash my hands. Looking up I catch myself in the mirror and stare into my own tired looking eyes. I look older than I should do; my skin looks thin and blemished. My throat is raw from shaving with a month old blade. I inhale/exhale and my shoulders sag.

I pass Donny Brinklow in the gents and he says to meet him in his office. Donny Brinklow powered ten hours a day by bottomless coffee and a thousand sucked down cigarettes. He used to be a branch manager at a rival store before Megamarket swallowed it up and he slotted in as a Department Manager on the immaculately conceived Megamarket pay grade scale.

I sit down in the non-dicking around chair on the proletariat side of the desk and wait there quietly to hear the outcome of my disciplinary procedure. I've had my fair share of bother in my time and I have this one pegged as a Written Warning. Maybe even Final. Basically I'm pretty sure that I'm alright here. A warning will stay with me for a year before evaporating away and then it's a do over.

To the right of me there is a big oak effect cupboard with the doors open, inside are three large CCTV monitors each one with its screen divided down into eighths and the pictures of all the cameras mosaicked together. Opposite this, on my left is the window with its neutral off white blinds half opened. Outside I can see the world split into sections; from here I can see the top of the wall that hugs around the yard and the stacks of dark clouds piling up on themselves. Maybe my Mum is right, maybe I am a vampire.

I hate the daytime.

"I'm moving you onto the day shift." Donny Brinklow says putting a fresh cup of coffee down onto a coaster upon his flawlessly clutter free desk. "And I'm going to give you a Written Warning for your language and attitude towards your Team Leader."

"Dayshift?" My shoulders sag some more and I feel as if I'm collapsing in on myself. Brinklow smiles grimly at me and says, "No, not really. But if I hear anything wrong about you then I'm going to pull you. Either onto days or out the fucking door." Sadistic bastard, you don't joke with a man about his days. "Do I make myself clear?"

"Yes." Flat voice, no backchat, nothing; like a freshly broken pony.

"As for the accusations of working whilst under the influence of drugs or alcohol."

"I deny that completely." I say a little loudly.

"We can't prove anything either way. It's word against word, so there will be no further action on that count."

"Okay, good. Thank you."

"Now, because I'm such a nice guy I'm going to give you two choices, you can either finish your shift today and start back on nights tomorrow, or you can go home now and come back this evening and make up your hours." Like choosing which testicle you want to have lopped off. Seven hours of Monday people or a free afternoon to have a drink or two before cleaning up and coming back. Customers or a hell of a dirty split shift. Customers or Sam Walters. Customers…

"I'll come back tonight."

"Fair enough. Get out of here."

I stand up and nod a goodbye and turn to leave letting my eyes drift over the screens within screens, there is always somebody monitoring something, we live in a world of screens. In every aisle of every shop, in every car park or public space, somebody is tuned into your channel. I open the door.

"Last chance, remember that." Brinklow says, looking up from his chair like that it almost looks like he has a neck. "Order yourself a new name badge, how is anybody supposed to know who you are?"

CHAPTER TWENTY FOUR

I arrive at my Mum's house at the same time as the Parcel Force man and I think Jesus Christ, what now?

"A new set of cups and saucers." She says as she excitedly runs the blade of the kitchen scissors over the brown tape.

"For all your tea parties?" I say sitting down and watching as bubble wrap and polythene paper foam out of the top of the box.

"You never know." She says, "That's what your father used to say." She says as she pulls out a thin china teacup with a photograph of the Queen printed cheaply on the side of it.

"Have you spoken to Rob recently?" I ask her as more bubble wrap comes out of the box.

"Not for a while my love, I think he's very busy at the moment." She's pulling out cup after cup each one with a different member of the Royal Family printed in the same low grade quality up the side of it. "Did you know that it's summer down there at the moment? They have their Christmas in the middle of the summer. Can you imagine it?"

"Sounds like a blast." I say glumly and stand up and go to the kitchen window resting my hands rest on the lip of the sink. Outside the garden is already looking beaten up by autumn; ragged patches of dead leaves are mouldering into the overgrown lawn. The birdfeeder is empty again and for a moment I think of Aunt Marie and Bonny and wonder how they're doing.

"Are you alright sweetheart?" My mum asks quietly looking up from fiddling with her new purchases. I know that she would ask me about the funeral and about Canada if she was able to. "Yeah, I'm fine mum. Just tired, that's all, just tired." I let my voice taper off to be replaced by the clacking of teacups being set in their saucers.

"Well that's alright then. It's good to be tired, means you're working hard." And then she stands up as if she's just decided on something. "Shall we have a cup of tea?"

"Sure, that sounds good. You stick the kettle on, I'm just going to go and feed the birds."

"Alright then. Your dad always used to say that tea tastes the best when it's drunk out of new china."

I open the shed door and step inside as a harsh wind blows the door to the reach of its hinges.

I could be in Uncle John's shed.

There is no wistful smile at the similarity between the brothers' sheds this time. This time I'm gripped by the cold realisation that maybe I'm still in Windsor, Ontario and that if I step back outside I would be back in Aunt Marie's backyard. It passes in a dizzy moment but it's enough for me to question my state of mind. It's enough for me to question everything and all at once in one overwhelming second before my hands grip the sack of bird feed and I return to myself grounded in a cold shed in Nowhere Town, England.

I carry the food outside and set it down next to the thin metal trunk of the birdfeeder which was setup and driven into the earth by my father and his mallet all those years ago. Taking out the plastic cup that rests at a soft angle on top of the grains and seeds I scoop out the feed and fill the wire mesh cylinders and reconnect their plastic tops. When each arm of the feeder is sufficiently replenished I pick the sack up again and return everything back to the shed without feeling any shared moment between my father and I.

Back in the kitchen my mum is sitting at the table, a steaming teacup in front of her as she scan reads the local paper.

"Yours is on the side my love, I couldn't remember if you take sugar."

"I take it how it comes." I say taking the cup and sitting down opposite. "How are you doing mum?" I ask sitting down and taking a sip out of Prince Phillip.

"Who, me? I'm doing fine sweetheart. I saw Debbie at my book club, she was asking about you?"

"Oh yeah?"

"Yes, she doesn't like the Stephen King though." Debbie used to live next door. I don't know where she lives now.

The doorbell rings.

"Who could that be?" My mum asks checking her watch and then standing up. "Back in a minute." She says turning and walking out down the hallway to the front door. I take another sip of tea and watch her open the door. Another guy in a Parcel Force uniform smiling and holding out a clipboard. My mum scribbles in duplicate and thanks the guy as he hands over a big flat square box.

"More stuff mum? Seriously?" I say as she fusses a space on the kitchen table and lays down her new parcel.

"It's a picture frame." She says grabbing the scissors and scoring the tape. "I'm going to sort out all the photos of us from when you were little."

"Well, I mean that's a nice idea mum but you have photographs of us all over the place."

"Yes I know but we have boxes filled with them up in the loft, I've been thinking about going through it for a while."

"Have you?"

"There is one thing, love, which I'd like to talk to you about." She says suddenly putting the scissors down and looking at me. "I've been thinking about your dad. I've been thinking that it might be time to, you know, let him go." She purses her lips together and I can see her trying to gauge my reaction. She seems lucid.

"What's brought this on?" I ask surprised at the words.

"Oh, you know how it is, I was just thinking about things, about life. Since your Uncle John passed away I suppose, I've just seen things differently." And then she's pulling the picture frame, unadorned thin black, out of the parcel and saying "I thought I'd make one of those collage things. With the photos I mean." And the conversation is closed.

"Well, whatever you think is best mum. You will tell Rob though, won't you?"

"Yes, of course I will sweetheart." She says fiddling with the clips on the back of the frame.

After a while I say goodbye to mum and walk to the bus stop and sit there just waiting. I don't even feel like smoking. Eventually the bus turns up and I see somebody watching me as I climb on and pay my money.

I get off the bus in the middle of town, same damp grey pavement pounded relentlessly by the same swarm with the hive mentality behind their eyes. I walk past The Crown and think about going inside for a few drinks but I've got something to do first so I blinker myself and keep moving forward.

The Arcade is a massive shopping precinct smack bang in the middle of town built as part of the perpetual regeneration programs that the people with the money like to initiate. It has shiny great walkways as wide as boulevards lined on both sides by mobile phone retailers and designer shops with their mannequins posed in funky ways and their tiny price tags. It all feels too clean, too precise. I try to avoid being sober in town. All around me everybody looks nearly identical; same haircut, same ironic jumpers, the same skinny jeans. This is the generation whose aspirations swish by in different shades of reality television, where the ideal is to be good looking and dumb and famous. I wonder how many screens I'm on.I haven't been to the public library since college but it looks exactly the same. It stands awkwardly attached to The Arcade by one of its plate glass walls with its entrance a little way removed. There is no money in regenerating a library. Naturally The Arcade is strictly non-smoking so the smokers; the skater boys, the stressed out executive types, the shopped out husbands and harried mothers all unite amongst the fag ends outside of the public library. Here they can congregate quietly, safe in the knowledge that the library staff are too timid to challenge them for blocking up their doorway. This is a good hangout for the beggars and buskers and tramps of the town, somebody out here always has some spare change or a smoke to bum. They all sit on the low wall that splits off an upwardly sloping walkway that leads to the multi-storey. I think about Johnny Wriggles and briefly scan their faces knowing that in all probability the whole

Colby Stein circus is at the other end of the country by now or maybe not even in the country at all. I flip the channel in my brain before those thoughts link up with others and push my way through the front door of the library.

The door closes behind me and suddenly everything is quiet. The librarian, an old lady with eyes like an owl looks up briefly from whatever it is that librarians do and smiles warmly.

"Hello."

"Hello."

"Do you need any assistance?"

"No, I'm fine thank you."

"Well, if you need anything, I'll be here."

"Thank you." I walk past the desk and through an old fashioned turnstile and a whole world of knowledge opens up before me.

I ignore it all and head directly to the computer suite. Only in a library can you get free internet access, well, I suppose you can in certain chain coffee shops too but only in a library will they give you the use of a computer as well. The computers are situated in a separate area from the main floors of the library. There are a few people, student types by their look, sitting around surrounded by open books and pages of notes, their faces screwed up as they squint their way through E-Journals or whatever time wasters the internet can tempt them with.

I sit down at the end of a line of monitors and wake it up.

I'm old enough to remember what things were like before the internet exploded the last years of the twentieth century. Somehow things didn't seem so disposable as they do today. When somebody took a photo you could touch it and hold it and get fingerprint smudges all over it. These days everything is in pixels and media files and everything is permanent but nothing lasts. We all exist now in some new dimension that was inconceivable to most twenty or so years ago. On the first day there was Tony Blair, on the second day there were mobile phones smaller than bricks and on the third day there was the worldwide web. The rest of the days disappeared in a haze of .com boom and child porn busts. The internet lost its innocence pretty fucking quickly.

I log on to Facebook and up and down my newsfeed are people's likes and dislikes and wants and hates and pictures of food. I notice how tense my shoulders are and force myself to loosen up. One new message. From Zara.

Are U OK?

I think about replying and my fingers even begin to tap out some words but I delete them and ignore the message. I take a steadying breath and navigate my way through various screens of settings and options until I find the one that I want.

Are you sure that you want to delete your profile?
Yes.
If you delete your profile you will not be able to get it back.
OK.
If you would rather we can suspend your account until a future date?
No.
You are sure you want to delete your profile?
Yes.

And all of a sudden I'm back at the front end of the website and I no longer exist. A surge of uncoupling relief sweeps over me and my shoulders relax. If I'm honest I don't really know for certain why I felt the sudden need to remove myself from the world's biggest social network, I just knew that it was something that had to be done. I step back out of cyberspace and lean back in the chair suddenly euphoric that at least part of my nihilistic self has finally been nullified.

Wiped out.

Gone.

CHAPTER TWENTY FIVE

Skin Tom hasn't turned up tonight. No phone call, no letter, no telegram. Myers prods the white ball up and down the length of the table playing a lonely game. Zeus is sitting at one of the tables behind me eating something that smells like melted plastic and cheese. I'm sitting in my usual seat in front of the television watching some well-fed men in pale suits rummage through the day's newspapers.

Samuel walks into the canteen and punches the combination for water into the vending machine. He takes off his glasses and wipes his brow with a paper napkin. With no Tom in the building he has had to pick up the slack himself. Out the corner of my eye I see him neck the plastic cup and order up another one.

"Has anybody heard anything from Tom?" He says to the room as he walks over and sits down a couple of seats away from me. He knows not to get too close. Nobody answers him, he looks over at me, I can smell the desperation on him mixing with the sweat. I ignore him and carry on watching the paper talk. Somebody holds up the Daily Flail which screams out some variation on immigrants and benefit cheats.

All of a sudden the red ticker bar at the bottom of the screen wakes up into capitals that say;

BREAKING NEWS: REPORTS OF AN EXPLOSION AT A MOSQUE IN TOWER HAMLETS, LONDON.

The camera cuts away from the fat men and back to the newsreader, some non-descript blandly dressed lady with plain features and a conservative haircut. "We interrupt paper talk to bring you a breaking news story; there have been reports of explosions at a Mosque in the London Borough of Tower Hamlets. Our reporter Brian Bland has just arrived at the scene and we are able to talk to him." The picture cuts to Brian Bland standing by a Police cordon, behind which Fire engines and Police cars can be seen with their blue lights flashing. Sirens are howling all about the night and the whole picture seems to crackle with tension.

"Well, Jesus Christ." Says Samuel, hovering behind my ear.

"You think he did it?" I ask and Samuel frowns at me briefly before refocusing on the screen. More sirens, more smoke. In the background the emergency services are a confused jumble of rushing uniforms.

"It's the Skinheads." Samuel says. "Got to be; that's changed the whole game." For once I agree with him.

"A new era for terrorism." Brian Bland says as his hair flaps in the breeze of the sirens. "Scenes of chaos here and nobody seems to know very much at all."

"This is very very bad." Zeus says. "Very bad."

Nobody says anything for a few minutes. Things are getting out of hand.

"It says on Twitter there are three bodies." Samuel says and his fingers twitch at his phone. "Stephen Fry is appealing for calm."

Brian Bland in his scarf at the scene. "Nobody knows what the cause of the explosion was, or indeed the amount of casualties if any at all." Oblivious as the internet refocuses its gaze and the web lights up. I'm thinking about long life cans of peaches.

I'm thinking about Defence League protests.

I'm thinking about people living without consequence.

Myers rolls the cue stick across the green top of the pool table and comes over and sits.

"The football highlights are on channel three."

"Nobody knows who to blame." Samuel says.

I stand in front of a wall of cat food, a wheel based table top laden up with Megamarket budget variety packs next to me.

These days there's a hostility in the air that wasn't there a few years ago, everything feels on edge. We cascade violently through the new millennium and everything seems to be falling apart. What once felt solid and defined now feels like its fracturing even as we watch through the windows of our digital boxes. Bombs and binges, the last days of Rome in wall to wall multiple angle replays.

Somewhere three babies are born.

Things were easier at University as if everyone was in denial about something. About everything. People still got excited about mobile phones. I didn't ever really think about the future, I just didn't think it would catch up with the moment, let alone blow past it. It was the end of the world after all; there wasn't any need for a life plan. I just didn't think that we'd last this long. But here we are and I'm off the pulse, missing the beat, lagging somewhere behind. Everything is now grimly laid out in front of me. My twenties are all roared out and what have I got to show for it apart from a toxic credit rating and a faded postcard of optimism.

Nothing.

Maybe Colby Stein has got the right idea; consequence is something to be avoided as a matter of principle, a lifestyle choice in you like. Colby Stein is crazy though.

The whole world is crazy.

I look out through the glass front of Megamarket and out across the car park. The same gaggle of every night cars knotted around the disabled bays near the front doors. A future outside of a supermarket seems a million miles away and anyway all I can see is a piecemeal, tepid world war and dead Father Christmas eyes.

CHAPTER TWENTY SIX

My phone vibrates on the table and dances itself to the floor. Half asleep, I stare at it for a couple of seconds, the bottle of wine, three quarters empty is balanced on my lap. I rub half a dream out of my eyes and lean forward to pick it up. Zara's name on the screen and my heart sinks a little. It's unusual that I fall asleep on the sofa. The television is muted in the corner; I'm still wearing my work clothes.

"Hello?" I answer it my voice cracking weakly on the 'lo. "Zara?"

"Guess again." Colby Stein's voice on the other end is calm and solid and unmistakable.

"Hello Colby." I search through empty cigarette packets until I find my current one and I tap a cigarette out and stick it between my teeth.

"I would like to see you."

"What time is it?"

"It's midday." His voice is patient but knows that what Colby wants, Colby generally gets.

"I don't know Colby. I have to work tonight; I was planning on getting some sleep in."

"I would like to see you." He says again this time his voice is a little harder.

"Why? What's this about?" I ask him although in the back of my mind I already know.

"It's about what happened in Canada." And he emphasises it with a silence.

"I have to work tonight." I find my lighter and set the flame to the cigarette.

"That's okay. I'm in town."

"Where do you want to meet?" I say resigning. My stomach has constricted and knotted I can feel the blood buzzing in my ears.

"Hope Plaza Hotel, two hours." He pauses again before adding. "I'm not fucking around about this." A thousand thoughts push themselves through my brain, jamming and snagging up against each other. I watch as the cylinder of ash grows along the length of the cigarette and as my hand betrays itself with a tremble the tube of grey dead carbon snaps off and falls to the dirty carpet.

"Okay." I say eventually, closing my eyes and sinking back into the worn out sofa.

"I'll buy you a coffee." Colby says and I can hear him smiling over the line. He hangs up.

Walking through town I don't feel so much tired as plain worn out. I can see the shadow men watching after me from every doorway and alleyway but I'm too beat for them to trouble me anymore than in passing. Passing The Crown I flip a cigarette end at one and it hisses as is sails through him and bounces against a wheelie bin and he disappears back into the gloom.

Since Colby's phone call I've been trying to gulp away the feelings of fear and nerves that rose within me when he hung up. It hasn't worked. I'm bothered that he wants to see me, more so I think because I have no idea what he wants to say to me. Surely he can't blame me for what happened? I wasn't driving the fucking car. Maybe Zara told him I was? I guess I'll find out soon enough.

I'm thinking about what my Mum said but at the moment I can't really figure out what to make of it. How to process it. She said that she wouldn't do anything until she had spoken to Rob and I know he'll say it's the right thing to do. And I also know that he'll come back, however fleetingly, for the funeral. But, I think to myself, maybe I've become worse at letting go than Mum herself. She copes by perpetually ordering junk and crap and living at a kind of standstill pace. But what about me? How do I cope? The more I think about the more I'm convinced that I've been living in my own personal kind of stasis. Maybe I've got it all wrong. Maybe I've been getting it wrong ever since I took that job at Megamarket. Maybe the boozing and the drug taking have hindered more than it has helped. There is absolutely no order to these thoughts that wind through my head.

And suddenly I'm standing on Hope Plaza looking at the same hopeless Hotel where this whole mess began.

Colby Stein sits in the bar at a table for two, facing the doorway with a newspaper folded in front of him. The emperor of consequence dressed in a dark suit with a black shirt open at the collar. He is wearing thin wire glasses and there is a pen in his hand, Sudoku or crossword I think to myself. He looks up and sees me and smiles broadly and puts the pen down. I nod at him and go over.

"Look at that," he says, "Two o' clock, bang on the nose. Please sit." And he gestures to the chair opposite him.

"You said you weren't fucking around. So here I am." I say, pulling out the chair and sitting down. He drops the pen onto the table and places his glasses on top of the paper. Sudoku. I fucking hate Sudoku.

"And I'm not." He says and he steeples his fingers in front of his mouth. "I haven't ordered anything. I didn't know what you wanted. I know you like to booze during the day…" And he lets it tail off and hang in the air like he knows some deep secret or other of mine. A pretty brunette comes over brimming with smiles and nice attitude.

"Are you ready to order?" So many teeth in that smile it doesn't look natural.

"Yes, I think so." Colby says and opens his hand out to me. I look him square in the eyes and say; "Three Budweisers and a double Jack Daniels no ice." Colby smiles at this like he's oh so clever and says. "Black coffee please."

"Sure thing, I'll be right back." And with a swish of her apron she's gone in perfumed efficiency.

"So, here I am. What do you want?" I ask inwardly cursing the smoking ban.

"Man, are you hostile." He says folding up his glasses and hanging them in his breast pocket.

"What do you want?" I say again without taking my eyes off of him. "You said it's about what happened in Canada-" I break off as the waitress comes back over with an organised tray full of drinks and a coffee.

"Would you like glasses for the Budweisers?"

"No. Thank you." Never trust anybody who pours a bottle of Budweiser into a glass. She lines up the bottles and the double Jack in front of me and places Colby's coffee next to his paper with a little pot rammed full of sachets of sugar.

"Thank you." Colby says and we both smile at her as she swishes off again.

"You said it's about what happened in Canada." I say again.

"That's right."

"Listen, I wasn't driving the damn car. Zara hit the kid." I hiss across the table at him. Colby doesn't react to me at all and picks up two brown sugars of which he tears off the tops and dumps them into his cup of steaming blackness. He picks up the spoon from his saucer and begins stirring. I drain half a Budweiser and put it back to the table with a little bit too much force so that it froths and bubbles up the neck.

"Whether you were driving the car or not driving the car is neither here nor there." He pauses, blows on his coffee and takes a delicate little sip. "The fact of the matter is this;" Another sip. "You're finger prints are all over that car and Zara's are not."

And a sudden vacuum fills my head, fills the bar, and fills the whole fucking hotel. And all I can see in the eye of my mind is Zara's hands inside Zara's gloves. Zara putting her gloves on. Holding Zara's be-gloved hand at the falls of Niagara.

Oh, Jesus.

Colby winds up one of those sickly fuck you smiles and takes another sip of his coffee. I can feel the blood rush out of my face all the way down to my feet and weight there leaving me swaying slightly in some non-existent breeze. I don't say anything and Colby watches me smiling quietly.

Oh, Jesus.

"What do you want?" I say clasping my hands together beneath the table to hide their shaking. Colby just takes another slurp of coffee.

"Of course you know that Canada and Britain are pretty tight, politically speaking I mean. What I mean to say is that if it was to come to light whose prints were on the car that hit and killed that poor little boy." He looks up at me. "You'd be gone."

"What do you want?" I say again and force my hand to lift up the half Budweiser to my face. And drink. I put it back on the table and pick up the Jack. Hard booze always tastes harder in the daytime.

"On Friday night something is going to happen at your store. What I want is for you to turn off the CCTV. And give me the keypad combination that's all. Nothing major, nothing big. Nothing that is going to kill you."

"You're going to rob it?" Reality slips slightly on its axis and everything seems a bit melted and surreal. I can feel the Jack Daniels behind my eyes and I'm not too sure of anything anymore. Colby picks up his newspaper and underneath it I see he has been hiding some kind of user manual which he pushes across to me.

"These are the instructions for the ISPY200 closed circuit television system that is in operation at your store. I've looked through it. It really is just a case of flipping a few switches. Easy."

"Jesus fucking Christ, you're crazy." I'm looking at the shades of grey user manual tauntingly laying there on the table, a perfect crease down its middle.

"There you go again." Colby says with a trace of malice now etched into his voice. "You're stuck in the mode of society, you're stuck man. There is no hope for you. You're destined to be a cog. After everything. Fuck me, I can barely believe it. After everything that life has shown you." He shakes his head and now I don't even know where the truth begins and where the lie ends. "I'm disappointed." He says. "I'm disappointed."

"You're crazy." I say again in the absence of anything more constructive or forward thinking to say.

"You're the one who's crazy. You turn thirty next month and you're still scabbing around for cheap drinks, you work a shitty job that you hate. You have nothing, your friends if that's what they are, look down at you like you're a crippled puppy. You're nothing but a fucking mascot." He pauses and takes a breath to control himself. "And still you go on abiding by these rules. You were born into a straitjacket and you're going to die in the very same one."

"Fuck you." I say as blandly as I can manage and take another drink. "What's stopping me going to the Police?"

Colby bursts out laughing so hard that he has to set his cup down in its saucer. "The Police? The Police go on facts. Facts like fingerprints and DNA. You'd be an easy win for them. They don't care about your sob story. They care about ticking off easy points and you my friend are an easy point." He clears his throat and begins dabbing at the coffee he's spilt with a paper napkin. "You're worthless to them and to all the power suits. Nobody gives a dead dog about a stacker. Wake up man. This is the real world and it's happening right in front of you."

Oh, Jesus.

"What's stopping you stitching me up down the line? What's stopping you blackmailing more out of me in the future?"

"Nothing. Nothing except that I don't care about you, I don't have any grudge against you. I have no further use for you after Friday. You go your way and I go mine. End of the story." He nods at me with a thin smile that says this is the best deal you're going to get.

"Okay." I say quietly.

"That's my boy." He says and he clinks his coffee cup against one of the beers. "Actually you're pretty lucky."

"Lucky?"

"You're lucky that your store operates such an antiquated system. It's easy work to earn the rest of your life back. Some hits we've pulled, things get a bit more complicated. Lucky." He nods as if satisfied with himself and picks up the newspaper so that it unfolds and he studies the front page. "Crazy world we live in." He says shaking his head and then he stands and drops the paper down on top of the ISPY200 user manual. He pulls a postcard of Niagara Falls from his breast pocket and tosses it over. "Keypad number." And he rolls a pen over. I shake my head and hesitate for a moment and then shake my head again and scribble out the four digit code. He plucks the postcard off of the table and pockets it.

"See you Friday." He says and pats me on the shoulder, "You can get the bill if you like."

And just like that he is gone leaving me staring at the screaming headline in front of me on the table;

MOSQUE SUICIDE BOMBER IDENTIFIED

and below it a passport style photograph of Skin Tom.

Stunned, I sag back into my seat and just stare at the paper. I hold my breath for I don't know how long, until black stars explode in front of my eyes. Eventually I breathe again and finish my drinks.

CHAPTER TWENTY SEVEN

They opened up Skin Tom's locker earlier. Two Policemen came down to the store to check it out, looking for clues I guess, or maybe a letter or something. All they found was his name badge and apron and tie. These all got taken away in polythene evidence bags, for some reason, I suppose to be filed away in some archive warehouse or wherever these things end up.

It's not been a very good week.

Everyone is very hushed tonight; nobody really knows what to say. Everybody is just leaving everybody else to their own thoughts. This is the sort of event that takes a bit of time to process, years perhaps, maybe it will never be fully processed but it is definitely one of those that you work through internally. It's surreal, like there's been some giant mistake somewhere, some catastrophic administrative error perhaps. This type of thought dances in and out of focus but in reality it's just froth, the substance is true.

Myers was so cut up that he had to go home, I don't blame him, how can you? Samuel asked me very politely if I would be okay to fill in for him over on Fruit and Veg. I told him sure, no worries. He even said thank you.

The Fruit and Veg come in on cages just like the rest of the stock but rather than mountains of cardboard packing boxes it comes in these green plastic trays. You know the ones; you see them in every Fruit and Vegetable section in every supermarket all across the world. IFCO trays. You take out the old, usually empty IFCO tray from the fixture and you drop in the new one freshly filled up at the depot.

Mangos.

Celeriac.

Loose Carrots.

1kg bags of Carrots.

There are two sizes of IFCO tray, full size and half size. All the different lines of carrots come in full size trays. The fixture for carrots looks like this; at the bottom you have a run of five IFCO trays of loose carrots. Loose carrots come in big polythene sacks within the tray and it is under filled. This means that they sit within the fixture two deep. In the tray underneath the sack remains sealed. The tray on top has its bag scored open in a cross shape by your yellow safety knife. The carrots must remain in their protective sack to maintain freshness. Immediately above the run of loose carrots is a run, again five long, of 1kg pre-packed. These are also under filled. Twelve bags per tray is twelve kilograms, times by five is sixty. Sixty times two is one hundred and twenty. One hundred and twenty kilograms picked up and placed in roughly five minutes. This is the sort of work that earns you callouses in the creases of your fingers. Makes your hands tough. My grandfather used to call it work worn. It keeps you honest.

Out in the smoking area I lay back on the bench with my feet up on the bike rack, this is where Tom and I sat not so long ago when he questioned his place in the world. The moon is high and bright and I look around it for any sign of an extra star but I recognise them all. I'm pretty sure that Tom's laid his own soul to waste. Crazy kid, I think to myself and shake my head. I'm aware of some movement behind me and to the left. I cock my head and look over.

"Hi." Samuel all sheepish in the shadows, I can tell by his magnified eyes that he doesn't feel comfortable.

"Samuel." I say. "This is regulation break."

"I know, I know." He seems all skitty and jumpy. "I just uh, I just came to check that you were alright." He comes out of the shadows and perches himself on the far arm of the bench. I smoke thoughtfully for a moment, not sure what to make of this.

"I'm alright." I say finally exhaling smoke into a plume which seems to catch a white blue in the moonlight.

"Pretty rough news." He says, "Pretty rough news." He repeats softly almost to himself and then sits down on the bench next to me. I throw my done cigarette into the scummy bucket and fish in my pocket for another.

"Do you reckon I could get one of those?" Samuel asks his voice thin and reedy and timid. I look at him surprised for a moment.

"Sure." I say and hold out the pack to him and he plucks one out. I do the same and pass him my lighter. He sparks up and stutters out a cough, smoke flooding his glasses and then his shoulders relax and drop as the nicotine massages his nervous system.

"It's been a long time." He says easing back on the bench.

"Well," I say, "I didn't know that about you." Samuel kicks his feet up onto the bike rack and gets into the smoking rhythm.

"I stopped when Gilly got pregnant." He says, "And that was what? Three years ago."

"Old habits."

"Old habits indeed." He echoes and then we sit there quietly for a couple of minutes. "I just don't understand why he would do something like that. I just don't understand."

"I don't either." I say but inside I'm thinking about Colby Stein and about what it means to be a consequence man. "I guess you never really know anybody. Not really."

"Fireman." Samuel says.

"What?"

"I always wanted to be a fireman." He says studying the end of his cigarette.

"Took a wrong turn somewhere." I say.

"Yeah, I suppose I did." And he sighs. "What about you?"

"What about me?"

"What did you want to be?"

"I don't know. I never knew." I think about the various ambitions that I owned at different parts of my life. I always had trouble moving through the different phases of my life. My parents used to say that it doesn't matter what you do in this world as long as you do it with pride, as long as you're happy.

"You must've wanted to do something though. Something other than this."

"I can't remember. I thought about teaching at one point."

"Really?"

"Yeah, once upon a time." Once upon a time was a long time ago.

"I can see you as a teacher." He says, I don't say anything. After a few minutes Sam goes back inside leaving me there, staring at the floating cigarette butts, thinking about the different turns I could have made.

CHAPTER TWENTY EIGHT

I sit on my head with my legs kicked back and curled over the top of the armchair. Like this I can see my Dad in a different way as to how he is presented to me, all waxy and deathlike. I watch him upside down for a good few minutes. After a while I flip myself off the chair and sit down on it properly, like an adult and still he lies there all blank and silent. Somebody, my Mum I suppose, has filled a vase with fresh flowers and set them on his nightstand. I don't know how often she comes here, two or three times a week I guess. Two or three times a week for twenty years is a hell of a lot of one way conversation. I wonder how she will fill her time after he's gone. All things told I'm glad that she has finally come round to the idea of switching him off but the timing of it has got me into somewhat of a spin, what with everything else going on at the moment. Still, they say the darkest hour comes right before the dawn. Maybe in a week's time, maybe in a month things will finally bubble down into some semblance of normality.

I'm thinking about my life and what Colby Stein had said. Can I really see myself stacking shelves ten years down the line? Twenty? But what else is there? My being, my entire being has become one with my job. I sleep, I drink and I stack the damn shelves, five days a week. I am Stacker and this is what I do. I turn thirty next month and all the people I grew up with have proper jobs and are starting to grow their own families and what do I have? A big fat nothing. I live pay check to pay check at the bottom of my overdraft. My credit rating has been flat lining for years. However you measure it I am not winning. But still there is something within me that just doesn't care about it too much. I mean there is some profound dysfunction within me that says that none of it really matters anyway. I should be a prime candidate to be a consequence man; I should be able to act out, guided only by my own personal limitations. Despite everything I just don't have it in me. This Friday Colby Stein and his group are going to rob Megamarket and I'm going to be helping them get away with it. This is worse than walking out of some two bit diner without paying for dinner. My first thought was to go to the Police but as Colby said the frame for that kid in Canada is squarely around me.

That kid in Canada.

There is guilt for that so sharp that every breath I take is like a razor blade etching a little deeper each time into the top of my stomach. I keep telling myself that I wasn't driving; it wasn't me that hit him and rearranged him into some defective looking doll, all limp and misshapen.

But you were there.

But I was there and nothing, not even a million prayers can ever change that. Another scar; another consequence. I wonder about Zara. Colby said she's all instinct but that has got to have messed her up. Hasn't it? Or maybe she saw the advantage of the situation and spun the plan to Colby. Johnny Wriggles was right alright, my life has definitely changed. My life has changed but my Father's has remained exactly as it has been for twenty years, unseeing, unknowing and beautifully passive.

For a moment I wish we could trade places.

When I get back downstairs Sandy is spraying air freshener over the plastic flowers. She stops when she sees me and smiles in that way that people do when there isn't much to smile about.

"How is he?" She asks in that way that people do when there isn't much to ask about.

"He's the same. Thanks for asking."

"Sorry, stupid question. How are you?" I like Sandy, she's alright. I'm half forming the words to say; *Yeah I'm fine.* But for some reason they don't get any higher than my gullet. I clear my throat and look at her all sagging shoulders and defeated eyes.

"You want a cup of tea or something? Maxwell brought in a super Victoria sponge this morning, I reckon I can nab us a couple of slices." You have to have a certain type of people perception to work in places like Haywoods. You got to be special.

"That would be nice. Thank you." I say my voice resonating with gratitude.

"Okie dokie." She says picking up the air freshener and putting it back in its cubby hole behind the table with the flowers. "Go and grab a seat in the lounge, don't worry all the guests are in their rooms. I'll be back in a couple of minutes."

The lounge is where the guests go to attempt to play board games and watch television game shows. Little tables are scattered all about with mix matched chairs around them. On the far side is a sliding set of patio doors leading out to a crazy paved terrace adorned at the corners with low maintenance planted shrubs. I sit down and out of the habit of sloth I put my feet up on the table. Sandy comes in carrying a tray with cups of tea and plates of cake, she pushes the door open with her generous behind and I automatically snap my feet off the table and rearrange myself leaning back in my chair.

"Here we are." She says with her friendly red cheeks, setting the tray down and sitting down opposite.

"This is all very kind of you Sandy." I say dumping sugar after sugar into my teacup.

"All part of the job," She says, "You and your Mum are regulars, long term regulars at that. Most that come through here are six monthers, a year at best."

"Yeah, I guess we've got a bit of a different gig going on." We both eject one of those little sad but funny laughs and sip at our tea.

"It must be difficult for you though."

"You get used to it. Like anything else, you get used to it." I stab my fork into the cake and take a generous bite. "When was mum last here?" I ask speaking through the food in exactly the way I wasn't taught.

"She was here yesterday." Sandy hasn't brought herself any cake.

"Yeah, I thought those flowers looked fresh. She's talking about flipping the switch." I say as casually as I can forking some more cake. I feel like I haven't eaten for half a life time.

"She mentioned it." Sandy takes a diplomatic sip of her tea. "How do you feel about that?"

"Well, I mean, I think it's the right decision but I've thought that since I was like ten. But…"

"But?"

"But it's been a rough little time."

"Have you spoken to your Mum?"

"No. And I'm not planning on it. I'm nearly thirty years old I can deal with my own problems. I just wish she could have reached this decision either ten years ago or further forward." I take a sigh and push the death of my cake away. "Timing can be a bitch can't it?" Sandy leans back in her chair and fixes me with serious eyes.

"Come with me." She says standing up nodding at me to follow her. She leads me back into the reception area and then jingles through a ring of keys hooked on her belt. She goes over to a door marked STAFF ONLY and inserts the key. I hesitate behind her but she motions for me to follow her. The other side of the door opens out onto a narrow dimly lit corridor. We turn left and walk down to the end. Sandy opens a door on the right and flips a light switch. Immediately I can smell something musty and stale. As I follow her in the smell intensifies. Inside are boxes and boxes of old paperwork, cleaning products, spare tables and chairs and at the far end of the room is a bed, exactly like my father's and on it lays a woman, ancient in appearance with a million deep wrinkles etched upon her face. She too, like my father, has a tube down her throat and various wires attach her to the same sort of machines that keep him ticking over.

"This is Molly." Sandy says. "She is one hundred and seven years old."

"Jesus." I say quietly. As I look closer I can see that the crevices of her face are coated with a fine layer of grey dust. "Why is she like this? Why is she here?"

"Molly has been in a coma since ninety nine. A deep coma. Not the sort that you come out of. Her husband was the only one with the authority to switch off her life support. He died."

"So what happens to Molly?"

"This is what happens to Molly. She stays like this. Not living but not dying either."

"How is this allowed to happen?"

"It happens more than you think. All the homes, places like this have these back room residents, it's just nobody talks about them. We call them the immortals."

"That is fucked up." I say genuinely staggered.

"It's a fucked up world." We back up out of the room and Sandy kills the lights and shuts the door. "So if your mum is getting to a point where she is ready to let go, it's probably best to let go."

CHAPTER TWENTY NINE

From the top of Maggot hill you can see out over the whole town. The thousand twinkle lights of yellow and amber play out across the whole sweep of it in private unknown dances. Anonymous beauty in streetlights and office blocks as below us a hundred thousand souls or more follow their own beats as dusk thickens and cloaks the sky above.

Me and Mike sitting up here, side by side like we used to do back in the college days. The small talk has played out now and I know Mike is on the verge of saying something substantial. I knew that something was playing on his mind when he called me up earlier and asked me if I wanted to go "up the hill." This is where you go when you need a bit of calm and perspective, where you go when things in town have got a bit too heavy.

"Helen's pregnant." He says it flatly and quietly.

"Shit, man." This is supposed to be good news. This is supposed to be what people want. This is supposed to be the point of it all. I know Mike though, I know his worldview, I know that a kid is the last thing that he wants.

"Shit, man." I say again.

"Shit, man is right." Mike says mating his hands behind his neck. "Helen is dead stoked. This is what she wants. This is what *we* want." Totally unconvincing. "It's just… It's just that's it now."

"You'll be a great dad." I say meaning it. "Just stop taking drugs."

"Yeah, I know, I know. The party's over."

"I think it has been awhile now."

"End of the party."

"New start."

"How are things with you? You seem kind of out of it." I could say a thousand things.

"I'm cool man. Just tired, having a bit of a draggy week." A thousand things wouldn't be enough.

And we sit in silence some more.

I miss being sixteen.

I miss being eighteen.

I miss being twenty one.

I can feel my shoulders sagging again and I make a conscious effort to stretch them back out and lean back on the bench. I wonder who this one is dedicated to. Specked with bird shit and occupied by two refugees of consequence.

CHAPTER THIRTY

Friday night and all around the world people are getting their rocks off. Maybe some kid in a University dorm is snorting some Vodka off of a teaspoon. Maybe skinny girls dressed in nothing dresses are puckering up for some date rape kind of hangover. Maybe old ladies are mourning the imminent passing of other halves. Maybe a lot of things are happening this Friday night.

Everyone at Megamarket is still going around in some kind of daze.

He used to be such a nice boy.

I just can't believe it.

Things like that, all sputtered out over milk dollies and thick cardboard packing cases. Nobody really knows where we stand anymore.

Already the Skinheads are celebrating Tom as some kind of hero. They call him a martyr. They say feed the Paki's some of their own medicine. They say meet violence with violence. They say the twenty first century was born in blood.

We're all going about our jobs the same as every other night. You pull the cage from the warehouse and you work the stock. We are Stacker and we just get on with it, we know no better. Only I do know better. I know that I have given Colby Stein the keypad combination for the back gate and I know that when I said that I was going upstairs to take a piss that I switched, in specific order, the whole ISPY200 system down so that it is useless and nothing. I know that over the course of the next seven hour shift my life will become forever changed and completely unchanged. I'm working down pet food. And every can of dog food with its beautiful smiling animal on the tin is a taunting reminder of some regular life that I'm never ever going to achieve or realise. All I can do is wait for the fucking storm.

Samuel is still maintaining his "I am your brother" way of coping. A deep part of me feels sorry for him. Fuck, I feel bad for everyone. I know what's about to happen. He doesn't even call me pet food. He calls me by my name. This is weird to me, I haven't been called by my real name for so long that it feels completely alien to me. I appreciate the sentiment though.

Megamarket is under the flight path of a few continental airplane routes. When a plane goes overhead you can hear it and it feels like the world is crashing down around you. Something about the frequency of jet engines smashes into the chambers of the rooftop and bounces around in such a way as it feels as if the plane is going to crash directly into the building. That mechanical wheezing cry. Screaming through the night until it passes and you're left once more with the flat sound of safety knife on packing cardboard.

I think I can hear that sound now, that low roar of jet engines.

And then the glass plated front of the shop explodes into a million fragments of flying glass and two black Range Rovers skid to a halt butting hard up against the cigarette kiosk knocking stacks of mesh baskets over like some crazy towers.

Here we go.

And all in one moment all the doors of the two vehicles are thrown open and seven, eight, nine people jump out all dressed in black with black masks and semi-automatic machine guns on straps on their hips and one of them screams.

"Get the fuck down on the floor."

And I know that they're coming in through the yard as well. I know because I gave them the keypad number.

Now the shadow men are moving up and down the aisles now grabbing Stackers and shoving them to the front of the store where they are made to lay face down all about the flower pod display fixture.

"One wrong move and I'll put a bullet in you." I know it's Ewan that's grabbed me and thrown me to the floor and I don't have the guts to say anything funny. "Give me a reason." He says jamming the barrel of the gun in my face.

Colby Stein walks down my aisle and despite his balaclava I can tell that it's him. His walk, his strut, his attitude of entitlement.

"Get up." He says pushing me with his foot. I stand up and he pushes me forward up the aisle until we reach the double swing doors at the back of the shop. Somebody already has Samuel with his arms locked behind him.

Somewhere an alarm is screaming.

"You're going to take us upstairs to the safe." Colby Stein's voice calm and solid without a trace of adrenaline. I can see that Samuel is sweating and has been crying; somewhere along the line he's lost his glasses.

"Okay. Okay." His voice is nothing more than a whisper. At the front of the shop somebody fires off a spray of gunfire into the ceiling. Somebody else screams. We are pushed through the double doors and out into the corridor where a row of cages of fruit and veg are lined up ready to go. They won't get worked tonight.

Samuel thumbs in the keypad code to the door leading to the stairs and again we get pushed through. Samuel stumbles on the first step and Colby Stein grabs him at the back of the collar and hauls him up.

At the top of the stairs I am pushed through the door by Ewan so hard that I fall forward and my shoes squeak and scuff along the tiled floor leaving smears of black rubber behind them. I get up and my heart is racing. I feel strangely detached from everything that's going on. As if I'm watching it all from somebody else's perspective. Ewan jabs me in the back with the gun and we carry on down the corridor towards the Cash Office.

Downstairs, more gunshots.

The Cash Office has the safe inside it and it has a thick reinforced door.

"I don't have the keys." Samuel says in a trembling voice.

"We don't need keys." Says Colby Stein and he takes something out of the black satchel that is slung over his shoulder. The thing in his hands looks like off white modelling clay. I've seen this before in movies. I know what it is. He goes up to the door and crouches in front of it moulding the plastic explosive into a mound around the lock. Once this is done he reaches back inside his satchel and pulls out a detonator. Behind him Samuel whimpers. Ewan smashes the butt of the gun into the back of his head and he crumples to the floor in a silent heap. Colby looks around and shrugs and then gets back to work with the detonator. "Get him out of the way." Colby says as he lights the fuse. I drag Samuel back around the corner with Ewan following with his gun trained on me. Colby joins us round the corner just as the explosion erupts spewing out thick smoke and the acrid smell of cordite. Immediately the fire alarm starts blaring, alarms on top of alarms. Colby looks at Ewan and says. "Five minutes."

Ewan looks at me and says, "Hands behind your back." I do as he says and then he spins me around and pushes my face hard against the wall and I can feel my hands being bound. Next thing he's kicking my feet out from under me and I land heavily on the floor the wind knocked out of my lungs. Samuel is groaning a thick ooze of blood seeping out from behind his ear.

The world is tilted and I'm looking at everything sideways. I watch them go into the Cash Office and a minute later there's another explosion and another bloom of smoke billows out into the corridor.

That detached surreal feeling.

Next thing I know Colby Stein is dragging me up onto my feet and is hanging two big holdalls around my neck. "Need you to do a bit of donkey work." He says and behind his mask I can see him wink. Ewan gives Samuel a vicious kick in the face snapping his neck and then slings two more holdalls over his shoulders.

"Let's go." Colby says and pushes me forward, my knees almost buckling under the weight around my neck.

Downstairs all the other stackers are lying face down on the tile guarded by four of the gunmen.

"Time to leave." Colby says and we hurry down the cereal aisle to where the cars are. Four others are already there loading the Range Rovers with canned goods and bottles of booze.

"Get in the fucking car." Ewan says as he hands his bags over to a couple of shadow men. He takes the bags off of my neck and throws them in the back. I do as I'm told, still feeling too stunned to speak.

Next thing I know is people are piling into the car all around me and doors are being slammed shut. For some reason I'm thinking about the time they picked me up from the train station.

Whoever is driving, has thrown the car into reverse and spun us back out into the car park, the other Range Rover follows almost as if synchronised. In the distance the wail of sirens cut through the night. And then we're gone, accelerating hard, due south, away from town and towards the motorway. As another one joins behind us.

Colby takes off his balaclava and looks back at me from the front passenger seat.

"Quite a buzz, huh?"

I don't say anything. Everybody else takes off their masks. I only recognise Ewan. We merge with the traffic on the M11 heading towards London and we slow down to regulation speed. I look around and see the second Range Rover join the middle of the night traffic a few cars back and also slow to a discreet speed. The third one is lost to the night and streetlights.

"We've just made a lot of money." Colby Stein says.

"Where are we going?" I say and there's fear in my voice. I think I might die tonight.

We turn off the motorway and into the dimly lit back car park of a rest stop somewhere near the airport, followed by the other two Range Rovers. Nobody has spoken for thirty minutes or so. The cars pull into adjacent bays and they kill the engine and the lights. Colby Stein sighs and nobody moves and then he opens his door and everybody gets out. The guy to my left pushes me out the car.

Everybody is moving in rehearsed synchronisation transferring the bags of cash from the backs of the cars into a dirty white transit van parked a couple of spaces over. I watch them dumbly as they hustle. Nobody even looks at me. Colby Stein appears at my side and watches his men at work. Ewan comes over and says. "Be seeing you." To Colby who just nods. Two of the Range Rovers pull away. Ewan and another guy climb into the van and drive away into the night. The night drops into a quiet stillness, there's just me and Colby and one other shadow man, smoking a cigarette by the remaining vehicle.

"And that is that." Colby says and he sighs again. "Come on." He says and puts his hand on my shoulder pushing me forward.

"Where are we going?"

"We're going forward." He says and we start walking. The shadow man by the car looks up and moves as if to come with us but Colby stops him with a shake off the head. We walk across the car park towards where the overnight trucks are parked up. Walking between them there is nothing but thick silence overlaid by the internal sound of my heart beat. I almost feel serene. We keep walking until we reach the perimeter fence. Wooden and rough with tangles of weeds and grasses twisted around it. I look at Colby who just nods in that way he does and we climb over into the field beyond.

"You know," he says, "It won't make any difference if you die tonight. Not really, not to anyone." He stops walking. "This is far enough." Its pitch dark here. The stars and moon smothered out by thick night time clouds. I can't think of anything to say. I imagine I'm facing up pet food.

"No difference. All you are is your memories and your dreams the rest of you is just particles and atoms and one day all that will be left of you is dust. Put your hands on your head." He says it so plainly that for a moment I don't react. And then there is the barrel of a gun against the back of my head. "Put your hands on your head." Calmly, quietly and I comply. "Kneel down."

So that is that then.

I kneel down and deep breaths shudder through my chest. It's in moments like this when you appreciate the finite value of everything you've ever known, the sheer soul crushing insignificance of everything.

"Anything you want to say?"

Ladies and gentleman it's been emotional. I get it now, I understand. I've blown it. Nearly thirty years of wasted oxygen. Should've been a teacher. Could've been a journalist.

"No, not really."

"Count backwards from ten."

"Ten."

Too old to be like Hendrix too young to be like Jesus.

Nine.

Will I feel anything, will I know?

Eight.

My flat is a mess.

Seven.

I hope they play Bob Dylan.

Six.

I'm sorry mum, I'm sorry Rob.

Five.

Four.

Where did my name badge go?

Three.

The next stage.

Two.

Fuck.

One.

I open my eyes and stare straight ahead into the blackness into the nothing and then I sneeze and I realise I'm not dead.

"Colby?" I say quietly. No answer, just thick silence. Slowly, I reach into my pocket and pull out my cigarettes and then a wave of sour relief washes over me and I start to cry and I lower my face to the dirt and curl up like some overgrown foetus in a Megamarket uniform.

After a while I walk back towards the rest stop. Between the dash-dash-dash line of overnight trucks the first blisters of sunrise creep through.

In the toilets of the rest stop I splash cold water over my face and look at myself through the grime of the mirror; darkly bagged eyes, hollow cheeks, no name badge.

Outside the toilets I buy an international phone card from a Polack in a tracksuit. The place is quiet and I walk across the tiled floor over to the bank of payphones.

I call Rob.

CHAPTER THIRTY ONE

He kicks his bare feet through the soft white sand and walks back up the beach towards the house that he rents from Jed. Behind him the Pacific Ocean laps quietly at the sands. Salt water drips from his hair. He can smell the sunshine.

When he reaches the decking of the beach house he turns back and looks out over the endless blue as a flock of gulls sweep between the sea and the sun and for a moment he thinks about his father. All those years and all those miles might as well be made out of the same thing.

He opens the unlocked door and goes inside and picks up his towel from the arm of the couch and drapes it over his neck. From the fridge he pulls out a frosted beer and cracks it open and takes a long drink, standing there with the refrigerator light beaming onto his tan.

Back out of the decking he sits down and leans back, kicking his feet up onto the rail. I'll never get bored of this view, he thinks to himself, the gold and the blue, the peace and the quiet. He puts the beer on the varnished wooden table and starts flicking through an old surf magazine. Maybe he'll invite the guys round for a Barbie this evening. Maybe he'll go downtown with Olly and find some girls. It doesn't really matter, it's all good.

Inside, the telephone rings.

"Hello." He says standing in the doorway.

"Rob, hey, it's me."

"Hey man, how you doing?" He says smiling and going back over to his chair.

"I'm okay." The voice on the other end of the line sounds quiet and somehow disconnected. How long has it been? He wonders.

"Yeah? It must be late over there." He looks at his watch. "Or early."

"I don't know, early I guess. What you been up to?"

"Not a lot man. Just been swimming, enjoying the sunshine."

"Sounds good."

"What about you?"

"Nothing much." In the pause he can hear the line crackle faintly. "Just stacking."

"When are you going to get out of there? It's not healthy."

"I don't know." Another pause, more crackle. "Hey, have you spoken to mum?"

"Not for a while, why? Everything okay?"

"Yeah, I guess."

"You guess?"

"She's been talking about switching him off."
The words bubble out of the receiver into his eardrum
and echo around in his brain and the dust blows off of
all the old memories that he stores there.

"Really?"

"That's what she said."

"Oh." And home suddenly feels very close and
as if on cue the sun dips behind a bank of clouds. "I'll
call her later."

"Okay."

"Is she still buying shit off the TV?"

"Yeah."

"Are you alright?" He asks. "You sound funny."

"I'm alright, just tired."

"You need to come off the night shift man."

"I don't like customers."

"Do something else. There's more to the world
than a supermarket you know."

"I don't know."

"You should think about it."

They say goodbye and Rob tips the last of his
beer down his neck and just gazes out at the long
horizon and remembers being younger on the other
side of world where, apart from in memory, the
sunshine was rationed and in the quiet moments you
can hear the ticking of your life.

CHAPTER THIRTY TWO

Two words keep on repeating in my brain. Like some mantra or some dirge.

Things happen sometimes and afterwards nothing can ever be the same. This is what they call life in the real world. Because that is all that life is really, a series of irreversible changes, constant progression. The good things and the bad just pile up on top of each other and leave you floating there in the present. Everything is transient, there is no constant. Mike and Helen will have their baby and in that time and place it will be the most beautiful baby that there's ever been.

Two words.
Two words.
Two simple words.

My father was cremated last week. My Mum finally let him go, burned him off this world. We scattered his ashes off of the end of the pier at Cromer and watched him blow away out into the murk of North Sea. Nothing and everything in the same instant and isn't that true of us all. A whole lifetime burnt down into nothing more than particles to be thrown and swirled in the air until they finally drop and become appropriated once more by the planet that we all share. The planet that keeps on spinning no matter what the consequences are.

And we all keep on spinning with it.

Rob came back for the week and we got drunk and talked about everything and nothing. I didn't mention Colby Stein. I didn't mention consequence men. We spoke of chasing footballs on beaches and piggyback races. We had a nice meal, the three of us, off brand new Royal family china.

Samuel has been off work since the robbery, stress and anxiety they say. Because I've been there longer than any of the other night crew they asked me to stand in as acting Team Leader, I said alright. Within a couple of days they had replaced the glass at the front of the store and changed all the keypad codes. And people carried right on buying. The Suits are thinking about turning us into a twenty four hour branch, they say to increase security.

I'm working down Pet Food again, nothing much has changed apart from every now and then I take a walk around and see how everybody else is getting on. So far there haven't been any issues.

Sometimes I think about Zara and about everything that happened and I wonder where she is now and what she is doing. I think about that kid in Canada and how his family must be. It still haunts me. I'll wake up from terrible dreams soaked in cold sweat. The usual.

I don't drink as much these days, most of the time I feel too tired. Even Pete Doherty is clean.

I'm facing up cans of dog food, each tin spun around so it's facing the right way with the pictures of Labradors and Border Collies lined up neatly and uniform. It's easy work and my brain keeps on repeating the same two words over and over, like my own personal metronome.

They say Samuel will be coming back to work next month. I don't know what he'll be like. The aisles are longer now and I'm not even halfway up.

And these two words keep on repeating.

Assimilate.

Conform.

The big hand scrapes around the clock picking up minutes and then dumping them out behind it. The stock comes in on cages that come in on the back of big Megamarket branded Lorries. The cages are lined up in the warehouse in rows corresponding to the aisles. The job of a Stacker is to fetch a cage from out back and work the stock up and down the aisle. The trick of the job is to take your mind out of it, let your arms and legs work, let your hands and feet guide. You can make it through a shift easy enough if your brain is elsewhere.

You daydream.

I am Stacker and this is what I do.

THE END

Printed in Great Britain
by Amazon